Chloe's March

by

Laura Pryor

Peggy,
all the best,
Laura

DORRANCE
PUBLISHING CO
EST. 1920
PITTSBURGH, PENNSYLVANIA 15238

Dorrance Publishing Co
585 Alpha Drive
Pittsburgh, PA 15238
Visit our website at *www.dorrancebookstore.com*

ISBN: 978-1-4809-6041-1
eISBN: 978-1-4809-6064-0

Years have passed since that chance encounter. Along the way, her styles have come and gone. Her once strong convictions have evolved. The young idealist who once saw only black and white now sees gray. She swore the only path was the straight one. She was popular with everyone. The spotlight shined on her and she welcomed it. During her freshman year of high school, she planned her future to the letter. She set goals and achieved them all.

Chapter One

For Chloe Conners, her achievements line the wall in her oak office. She graduated with honors and returned to her hometown of Portland. The eight years since graduating high school have rapidly blown by. She finds herself sitting in solitude and appreciating her success. She is assured of being a full partner within a couple years. She was made junior partner two years ago. Chloe's telephone rings.

"Chloe Conners, how can I help you?" she asks in her strong, focused tone.

"It's me, are we still on for dinner?" her fiancé inquires.

"Hello, Craig. Yes, dinner is a go. How's your day?" she continues while opening a folder.

"Long and tedious, and yours?" he returns the question.

"Fine! Dinner at the usual place?" she inquires.

"Yep, see you at eight," Craig states.

"See you then," she answers. Chloe continues reading files and preparing her findings.

Meanwhile, across town a hand closes a photo album filled with clippings of Chloe.

As dinner time arrives, Chloe finds herself at the usual restaurant waiting for Craig. As she sits in the center of the room at her normal table, a person resembling her past walks by the window. She is mesmerized by the sight of her perceived past. Chloe is taken back and speechless as her waiter hands her a message. The young man clears his throat to gain her attention.

"Miss Conners," he speaks handing her a message.

"I'm sorry, Allen, yes?" she says watching her past walk by.

The message reads, "Sorry honey, a last-minute meeting. See you tomorrow. Love, Craig"

"Thank you, Allen," she says. She allows the usual cancellation to roll off her thoughts. Chloe pays her drink tab and leaves.

The mist begins once more as she emerges from the restaurant. Her slender hand summons a cab as she fights the urge to look for her past. The cab interrupts the search her blue eyes had begun to make. As her hand closes the car door, she shows a slight smile. While the cab streaks through town, Chloe's memories spark images of the past and present as the street lights zip by. She fights the past knowing the irreparable harm it can cause to her present and future. The cab stops in front of her downtown apartment building. The doorman opens the secured door for her. Roger Elms has been in his present position for fifteen years. His stout build and polite gestures reflect the person he always was. Roger was a high school chemistry teacher. He retired at the age of fifty-two. Within a couple years, he found himself bored and lonely after his wife passed.

"Thank you, Roger," Chloe says tipping him.

"You're welcome, Miss Conners," he replies.

"I think the oncoming storm is going to pound us tonight," he comments pushing the elevator button for her.

"Roger, I think you may be right," Chloe answers as thunder crackles off the coast line.

"Well goodnight, Miss Conners," he states as the polished doors open.

"Goodnight Roger, and please do call me Chloe," she remarks.

He tips his cap in a *yes* gesture and smiles.

The bell dings as her floor arrives. Her apartment is on the southeast side with a picturesque view of Mount Hood. Chloe dims the lights in her hallway as she approaches the bedroom. The glass doors on the ceramic tile shower steam after she turns the faucet on. Stepping out of her black suit, her small feet sink into the plush carpeting as she returns to the shower. The hot steam reawakens the day they first met at church camp.

Chloe was surrounded by friends as they spent their last year there. Her eighteenth birthday is two weeks away. Her senior year begins after that. With the lower attendance at camp that year, three churches combine on the same weekend. Chloe and her friends since grade school giggle as they join the rest of their group. Chloe and three others are assistants to the camp counselors. They were assistants last year as well. The three groups are huddled together on opening day. Two-thirds of the campers are strangers to Chloe and her group. Nonetheless, she enjoys the spotlight as the introductions are made. The warm sun soaks her blonde hair as her tanning bed skin glows. Each group has three assistants. The three churches each have about twenty-five members attending. The assistants are buddied with each other and are assigned their own group. Chloe and her best friend are buddied. Their group is known as group red. The other groups are blue, yellow and green. As they lead group red to their cabin, Chloe and Heather Meager assign cots to their group. They introduce themselves to their group. Within the red group, Chloe and Heather split the group in half and assign themselves to a smaller group. When day one winds down, the assistants sit by the fire. The twelve of them become friendlier when Chloe makes a strong statement.

"We are Group Red and we are going to win every challenge!" her confident attitude declares. Her confidence is met with a defining remark and followed by a long stare.

"We'll see!"

"I don't believe we have met," Chloe sharply states as her confidence is challenged.

Her remark is countered by a coy smile as the challenger simply leaves the meeting and retires for the evening.

The water turns cold and her remembrance ceases.

Her silk chemise slides over her perfect form. She lets her soft feet glide over the hardwood leading into the kitchen. Pouring a glass of merlot, she returns to her sanctuary. The light gray walls are splashed with colors from various artwork. Her black satin sheets are cool to the touch as her long legs slip between them. Chloe allows the storm to relax her as she stares out the private balcony. The lightning illuminates the snow cap of Mount Hood as the thunder clasps grow closer. The thunder draws her from the resting position. Chloe opens the sliding door and steps out onto the balcony. She has always loved watching storms.

The wind blows her gown as she leans over the railing. With the sharp breeze forcing her shoulder length blonde hair over her deep blue eyes, her eyes close as the scent of rain and forest tantalize her senses. As a raindrop crashes on her blonde hair, Chloe decides to retire for the evening. The past she met tonight flashes in her dreams. The satin sheets twist with her as she tosses.

Chapter Two

The morning peaks through the hovering clouds. She awakens tired and confused. The dreams linger as she showers and begins her normal routine. She has maintained her sleek figure since high school. Chloe stops at a local coffeehouse before heading to work. She normally brews her own.

"Good morning, Chloe," the barista says.

"Good morning, James," she answers. Latte in hand, she turns to leave. As her phone rings, Chloe shuffles her drink and briefcase to answer. "Chloe Conners speaking, how may I help you?" her professional tone speaks.

"Jacob here, we have new client. Are you available at nine-fifteen?" he asks.

"Yes, I have an eight-thirty, but that shouldn't take long. I will be there in a few," she states.

"Thank you," he responds.

Jacob Long is the founder and senior partner in the firm. He is also her mentor and friend. He has sponsored her for full partnership. His fatherly hovering has protected her from the office drama and squabbles. She quickens her pace before the rain begins once more. He is a large man with an even larger personality. He is slightly shorter in comparison to Chloe, but his personality and love of pranks polarizes the office and most new clients. He is a walking contradiction to the law community. The firm specializes in corporate and constitutional law. Chloe was courted after graduation by the firm. As she enters the pristine office, she relishes the day her name will appear on the door.

The firm may be small in comparison to the others in Portland; however, it is highly regarded. She is greeted by everyone she passes. As she closes the door behind her, it quickly opens.

"Good morning, Chloe," her secretary Taylor Clemons says.

"Good morning, Taylor. Can you pencil in a nine-fifteen meeting with a new client?" Chloe asks placing her briefcase on the pine desk.

"Sure can. The file for your eight-thirty is updated and on the desk. Let's hope he is done merging for the year," her voice remarks.

"I agree," Chloe replies as Taylor leaves.

She begins to review the file Taylor placed on the desk. As the sunrise continues to ascend, Chloe walks to the break room. She is met by Stanley Wayne, the other partner.

"Good morning, Chloe. Is the merger king done for the year?" he inquires.

"His money is welcomed, but he is such a gross little man," Chloe responds before reaching in the refrigerator.

"That is precisely why I passed him off to you. The first meeting with him and those rude grunts and belches was enough," he states leaning against the counter.

"Thanks, I think. Do you know anything about this new client and the nine-fifteen meeting?" she asks hoping for any insight.

"Not much. Only that he requested you," he states.

"Me? Why specifically me?" Chloe asks as she places a bagel in the toaster.

"Not sure, but Jacob and I were very intrigued. Oh well, we'll soon find out!" he says before leaving.

Chloe makes her way to the conference room and prepares for her first client. Taylor joins her.

"Do you want Curtis to sit in with you?" she asks referring to her clients' hands on tactics.

Curtis is an intern.

"Nope, that is why I chose the glass room. Can you make sure to interrupt me at nine? I think thirty minutes with him is about all I can take in one session," Chloe all but begs of Taylor.

"Sure thing," Taylor remarks as they head toward the entrance to greet him.

As Chloe stands impatiently waiting for her first client, she thinks back on dinner last night.

Her daydream slips away as Charles Norman enters. (Charles Norman is a self-made man in his own mind. Chloe loathes his wealth and self-entitled ways. His ill-mannerisms are a direct result of the "short-man" syndrome.)

"Good morning, Mr. Norman. How are you today?" Chloe asks hiding her disgust for him.

"Good morning to my favorite attorney," he speaks before touching her arm.

"Right this way, Mr. Norman," Chloe offers leading the way to the conference room.

He takes the seat across from Chloe.

"So, what can the firm do for you this time?" she asks hoping he will remain seated.

"I am considering expanding my real estate holdings into Eugene. There is a local realtor looking to retire and approached me about buying him out. Can you investigate this and come up with an appropriate offer?" he asks as his legs lift him and her hopes are about to be dashed.

He walks around the table and approaches her.

"Yes, I will investigate this. Is there anything else you need?" she asks not realizing he is circling the table.

He stands behind her and caresses her shoulder before speaking.

"This is time sensitive and we can always talk about it over dinner," he suggests as his pudgy fingers rest on her shoulders.

Her reaction is quick and concise. "Don't touch me like that again!"

"Oh, sweetie, I am harmless," he remarks taking a step back.

Taylor knocks on the door to interrupt the meeting.

"Come in!" Chloe says.

"Excuse me, Miss Conners, your nine o'clock is here," Taylor says.

"Thank you, Taylor," Chloe responds.

"I will be in touch when I have an offer," Chloe exclaims with disgust.

Chloe shows him to the door and heads toward her office.

She instantaneously rushes to her private restroom. She can feel his grime and slime on her hands and shoulders as revulsion overcomes her. Chloe immediately scrubs her hand and sanitize them afterward. She places a few calls regarding Mr. Norman's request. As her next appointment arrives, Chloe receives her messages from Taylor before heading to her next client. Jacob and Stanley approach Chloe as she walks to the entrance.

"I love the idea of a new, unknown client. It is sort of intriguing," Jacob states.

"Yeah, if he is not a hands-on type," Chloe remarks as her next appointment stands to greet them.

"Good morning, Mr. Griffin," Jacob says offering his hand.

"Gentlemen…and Miss Conners, I presume?" the tall, slender, fair-haired man says.

"Good morning, Mr. Griffin. Please follow us," Chloe suggests leading the way.

As she pours a glass of water for him, he remains quiet.

"I understand you requested me?" Chloe inquires.

"It is to my understanding that you are very competent when it comes to contractual issues. My client has such an issue," he remarks as his stature remains stoic. (He is closing in on the higher end of middle-age. His sandy brown hair is becoming speckled with white. His tall, mousy frame and narrow cheeks enhance the aging appearance.)

"So, you are not the client?" Jacob asks with confusion.

"Yes, that is correct! I am merely a representative of my client," he states.

"This is a bit unusual. Nonetheless, how can we assist you?" Stanley states.

"Good, let us begin. My client is considering a buyout. However, no official offer has been made. We are a larger company wanting to move into Portland. We have met with resistance from the city council as well as the mayor. They do not want my client to partake in the Portland area revenue. This file explains our initial plans and our business model. My client will be grateful for any insight or assistance with the handling of this problem. Here is my card. All correspondence will filter through me. Do you have any questions?" the mysterious man asks.

"At this time, there are no pertinent questions. I am sure we will have some," Chloe confidently adds.

"Good. Then I am expecting a standing appointment for every Monday until this is resolved," the soft-spoken representative remarks.

"That is not a problem," Chloe states.

"If there is nothing else I must be going," he adds before standing.

"No, I think we are good for now." They shake hands and escort him out.

With the file in hand, Chloe rushes to her office.

Stopping at Taylor's desk, Chloe makes a few requests.

"Hey, Tay, please hold all calls except for family and Craig," Chloe says as she thumbs through her existing messages.

"No problem, Chloe. You have one appointment late this afternoon. Do you need me to reschedule this?" Taylor asks.

"No, it is with Joseph Rands. This is just to sign a few documents," she nonchalantly states.

Chloe disappears into her second home. The morning passes quickly. Chloe is completely entrenched into this mysterious client. Lunch time arrives, and her appetite does as well. Taylor walks in unnoticed as Chloe is buried in the research for the new client.

"Hey, are we still on for lunch?" Taylor asks leaning over Chloe as her strawberry-blonde hair slips over her green eyes.

Taylor waiting for an answer grows impatient. She drops a pencil on the file in front of her boss.

"Oh sorry, I was lost in this mystery. Is it lunch time already?" she asks.

"Yes, are we still on for the lunch?" Taylor asks.

"Yes, considering it is your treat," Chloe sharply states.

"How is it my treat?" she asks.

"Because you were late interrupting my meeting this morning," Chloe sharply answers.

"Oh damn, I hoped you hadn't noticed. I was enjoying watching you squirm as he touched you," Taylor smirks after her response.

"He is a slime ball," Chloe states as she slides each arm into her jacket.

They step out of the office and head toward a local diner.

With an uneventful lunch filled with office gossip, they return to finish their day. The late appointment is handled quickly, and Chloe leaves early. Inside her burgundy leather briefcase is the file from the new client. She arrives home to find a moving van stopped in the loading zone.

"Good evening, Roger. What is the info on the new tenant?" she asks handing him a tip.

"The tenant is on your floor on the opposite corner. That is all I know," he exclaims while holding the door for her.

"Wow, someone new to the floor! Great, I have to break someone else into my rules," Chloe sarcastically remarks with a coy smile.

"Yes, ma'am," Roger says as elevator doors close.

The modern apartment welcomes her after a unique day. Chloe undresses and finds her favorite shorts and tee shirt. She opens her briefcase and begins to review the file once more.

Her focus is interrupted by loud voices in the hall. Trying to drown out the annoying voices Chloe retreats to the balcony. The noises cease and quiet returns. She begins to research the company the man represents. She hits one road block after another researching the parent company. Each company is part of another subsidiary. She writes on a post-it and circles the company name the others are tied to. The name is Sycamore Services. She stares out into the darkening sky and finds satisfaction in her discovery. The knock on her door disrupts her satisfaction. She opens it to find Craig holding take-out.

"Hi honey, thought we could do take-out," he childishly suggests.

"Well hello! Come on in. I am hungry," she says with a smooch from him. Her round hands and fingers rest on his muscular chest as his arm pulls her into him. They share their day and the Korean dinner. As the evening turns late, they prepare for bed. He acquires a passionate moment she does not offer.

Chapter Three

The morning arrives quickly.

"Are you going to volunteer at the camp this year?" Craig asks as he dresses.

"Yes, I always look forward to the escape. The laughter and carefree of the two weeks seems to energize me," she answers slipping on her heels.

"What are you doing those two weeks without me?" she inquires.

"Think the guys are going to the Seahawks training camp or something like that. They offered, and I accepted," Craig joyfully answers.

"What about the second week?" Chloe asks as she files her paperwork into the briefcase.

"Nothing but catch up. I am sure of that," he replies. Craig is a corporate attorney for another law firm.

"When do you leave for camp again?" Craig asks as he sips on juice.

"In a couple weeks," she responds as her hands straighten her jacket.

As they step from her apartment, Chloe notices a hand sliding on a door before disappearing into the newly occupied apartment down the hall. Her thoughts are running parallel with her intrigue about the new neighbor. They say goodbye at the door of the building and leave in different directions.

Her normal routine and latte carry Chloe into her office. She spends the morning looking into the business plans listed in the file from yesterday. She calls the mayor's office hoping to have a copy of the previous meetings notes faxed to her. She finally returns her mother's call from two days ago.

"Hello, Mother. How are the two of you?" Chloe sweetly asks. She applies a sweet tone hoping to avoid a tongue-lashing her mother usually gives when she forgets to call back the same day.

"Who is this?" Ruth's persnickety tone asks.

"Sorry, I was late calling you back," Chloe apologizes in a surrendering tone.

"That's okay. One of these days your return call will come too late!" Ruth angrily states.

"Okay, enough of the guilt. I get your point. So, how is everything?" Chloe asks.

"We're fine, dear. Are you going to participate at camp this year?" Ruth inquires as her tone softens.

"Yes, I will be a counselor this year. I wish Heather could be there. We haven't seen or spoken to one another in months," she remarks.

"Barbara Meager sends her thoughts," Ruth responds.

(Barbara Meager is Heathers' mother.)

"How is her marriage?" Chloe asks knowing Heather and her husband hit a rough patch last year.

"Heather and Rick are getting a divorce. Heather told me that he cheated on her. Heather is moving back after the divorce is final. She and the two children are moving into David and Barbara's guest house," Ruth states.

"I guess I should have returned her call. I just forgot or got busy," Chloe says trying to squeak pity from her mother.

"Glad to know you don't call *anyone* back," Ruth sarcastically remarks.

"Are we still on for dinner Friday?" she asks.

"Yes, if you do not cancel," Ruth comments.

"I won't. I got to go. Love you guys and I will meet you at the restaurant at seven sharp," Chloe confirms.

"Love you, dear. See you Friday," Ruth ends the conversation.

A knock on the door interrupts her thoughts. Taylor hands Chloe the fax she requested.

"Chloe, do not forget your ten-thirty," Taylor states before leaving.

"Can you give me a call around quarter after?" she asks her best friend Taylor.

"Sure thing," Taylor answers.

Chloe reads the fax and wonders why the business license was denied. Her thoughts wonder back to the mysterious client and why they were not mentioned in the file Mr. Griffin handed her. She reads and re-reads the file hoping something was missed. With frustration looming, she closes the file and prepares for her next client. The rest of the day drags by and her thoughts return to the file.

With the arrival of evening, Chloe stops at her favorite Chinese restaurant. She places her order and looks at a message on her phone. In the meantime, a black limousine stops across from the restaurant. The window is cracked as the occupants watch Chloe.

"Is she intrigued by the file?" the person asks.

"Yes, shall I cancel the next two meetings with her?" Mr. Griffin inquires.

"No, let her call you. She will have Taylor place the call. Do not accept Taylor canceling the meetings. Only speak with Chloe. When she does call, tell her you understand, and your client will await her return in two weeks," his boss adds.

"Will do. Are you going to show up at the restaurant Friday?" he asks.

"No, I need to clear my schedule and wrap up some loose ends. I will not see you for two weeks. Just keep investigating. I want to know everything," the strong voice states.

"Yes, I will keep you posted," his words confirm.

"Good, I am about to topple her perfect, confident world," the boss states as a slight grin shuffles in Chloe's direction.

The limousine drives away.

Her awaiting cab escorts Chloe to her empty apartment. As she exits the elevator, Chloe notices her new neighbor's door close. With her flute filled with white wine, Chloe twists her fork into the noodles. Page after page of contracts, Chloe finally reaches the end. With her eyes squinting and burning, she showers and ends the night after midnight. The next three days are pressed with meetings. As Friday evening arrives she is excited to see her parents and enjoy a relaxing dinner. She meets them at their restaurant. Her father Ray opened it in the late nineties. He is an award-winning chef. Her mother was the accountant. They no longer take part in the day-to-day operations. His managers handle the daily business. Once a week, he will inspect the cleanliness and preparation of his kitchen. His free time affords him the opportunity to create new recipes. Her mother, Ruth, inspects the books and payroll. Ruth's once slender body is now becoming full as her age increases. Her light brown hair and fair complexion highlight her crow's feet. Her round face and oval glasses finish out her next-door-neighbor look. She had spent many long evenings helping Ray build his restaurant. During the day, she would spend much of her time as a CPA. Ray's once blond hair is fading into white. He strong jaw line and thick chest have not changed. Ray met Ruth in San Diego thirty years earlier while on shore leave. They married two years later. After his Navy stint, Ray returned to his passion. His love of food was instilled in him by his Sicilian grandmother. He was the light in her eyes. She taught him everything he knew about the kitchen and cooking as an adolescent. They moved in with his fathers' parent's, and his mother worked outside the home when his father died at the age of thirty-two in an automobile accident. She helped put food on the table and he learned to cook. His father was Irish and his mother, Nicolina was Sicilian. They met in New York and married. Though, she learned how to cook Irish cuisine, Nicolina favored Sicilian. Like his mother, Ray was an only child. Chloe never knew her grandmother. She passed away shortly after Chloe's birth.

The aroma of freshly baked bread awakens her hunger. She is greeted by several staff members. Chloe's high heels click on the tile as she is shown to her table. Her parents are waiting for her.

"Hello Mom and Dad! It is good to see you again," she remarks after kissing them both.

"Hello darling, where have you been keeping yourself? Your mother said you had forgotten to return her call," Ray says in a soft yet stern voice.

"I am so sorry. I was just handed a new client. For the last two days, I have been swamped with meetings," she answers trying to apologize.

"I understand, sweetie. We all get busy from time to time," his smooth voice replies.

"Where is Craig?" Ruth asks.

"He is out of town," Chloe states abruptly.

"Is everything okay between you two?" Ruth asks hoping to pry.

"No, we just have not seen much of each other. You know how it goes," she says referring to the fact that her father was missing from most of her childhood as he was building the business.

They both nod.

"Ruth said you are going to be a counselor this year?" he asks.

"Yep. I always look forward to going there," Chloe remarks with fondness.

"Do you remember that year at camp and how your team lost to the other group?" Ray reminds her.

"Yes, and I also remember how mad I was," Chloe answers as regret filters into her tone.

"Oh, you have always been so competitive. For goodness sake, it is just camp!" Ruth exclaims as their waiter arrives.

The three of them order and reminisce for hours.

Chapter Four

Chloe sighs as her weekend ends when the alarm on her nightstand rings. She has a hectic week ahead and four days to fit everything into. With her morning routine behind her, Chloe summons Taylor to her office.

"Morning Chloe, how was your weekend?" Taylor as a smile follows her.

"It was too fast. We have to organize my schedule and change or cancel appointments, so have a seat!" Chloe exclaims.

"Okay, you have eight appointments this week. Today you have three. Tuesday and Wednesday, you have two each day. Thursday there is only one at eleven. What are your instructions?" Taylor says reciting her schedule.

"Okay, keep the three today. Cancel Mr. Griffin's next two standing appointments. Tell him I am still looking into the city council and who can assist us. Keep my follow-up with Mr. Rands. I always look forward to seeing him. Wednesday, keep the two appointments. And for Thursday, clear my appointments. I cannot take another week of Mr. Norman. On the week I return, schedule meetings every day until I am caught up. Any questions?" Chloe asks.

"No problem," Taylor answers.

"Okay," Chloe says.

Taylor immediately begins freeing her schedule. She calls Mr. Griffin.

"Hello, I am calling on the behalf of Chloe Conners. Mr. Griffin, she is needing to cancel the next two appointments," Taylor states.

"Taylor, that is your name correct?" his monotone voice speaks.

"Yes Sir, it hasn't changed," she politely response.

"Do not take this wrong, but I expect her to call me. So, she will have to call me," he strongly states.

"Okay, I will let her know. Thank you for your time. She is going to flip," Taylor says.

His voice chuckles before ending the call.

She rushes into her boss's office to inform her of their conversation.

"Chloe, you will not believe the call I just had!" Taylor says with excitement.

"What call?" Chloe inquires.

"I called Mr. Griffin to cancel your next two appointments. He said he expects you call and not me!" Taylor says with amazement and anticipation at her boss's response.

"You're kidding me, right?" Chloe says looking up from an open file.

"Nope. So here is his number. Have fun with that call," Taylor says as she walks out.

Chloe does as his boss said she would.

"Hello Miss Conners. I am glad you called me. I understand you will need to cancel my next two appointments," he states.

"Yes Sir. I am looking into your client's situation with the city council and hoping to find someone to assist us," she explains.

"No problem. Thank you for the update. I look forward to seeing you in two weeks," he explains before ending the call.

As her intrigue builds, she tries to focus on her other appointments. Finally blocking the mystery from her thoughts, Chloe's busy week begins. She dispenses with each meeting and respective day. Finally, Thursday night arrives, and she finds herself at home looking out at Mount Hood. Her memories carry her into the past and the night her challenger walked away from the campfire comes to mind. When the fellow assistant walked away, Chloe was unaware of the brutality her ego was about to sustain. After retiring for the evening, her thoughts ran wild at the ease in which a stranger shook her confidence. She was about to enter unfamiliar territory.

The bright sunny morning finds her groggy. Chloe yawns and stretches trying to awaken herself. The team is filled with excitement and energy. They meet in the dining room after showering.

Chloe and Heather follow their team into the dining room. Her blue eyes immediately search for her challenger. As they see their target, Chloe is somewhat taken back at her challenger's interaction with the group. Her challenger is sitting next to a small boy. He looks small for his age. The minimum age for the camp is eight. The toe-headed boy looks six. Her challenger is giggling with him. Chloe continues in her steps as she follows her group. As their breakfast is being consumed

Chloe's careful glance catches her challenger's attention. Her challenger smiles and leads group green out.

The green group heads for the painting and drawing center. Chloe's group passes the painting center. She cannot resist the urge to glance at her challenger once more. Their eyes meet, and Chloe quickly turns away. Five days into the first week and her challenger was reassigned to the yellow group due to an illness.

As she turns away, the cool night air returns her to present day. A loud noise down the hall startles the quietness her apartment has come to know. Opening the door, she looks toward the end of the hall. Her blues eyes catch a glimpse of high heels entering her new neighbor's apartment. The noise ceases as the door closes. She is becoming annoyed with the elusiveness of her new neighbor. She shakes her head as frustration builds. Chloe returns to her apartment.

Chapter Five

S he awakens to a bright new day. She is filled with excitement at the thought of her yearly adventure. After packing, Chloe makes her way to the parking garage where her silver SUV is stored. She drives it a few times a month. She uses it for a weekend excursion to her cabin on the coast. Tossing her luggage in the back, she returns to her apartment. Chloe packs a small cooler and snacks. After securing the apartment, she heads for the elevator. As the doors begin to close, a hand bumps them open.

"Oh, hello Chloe," her longtime neighbor says.

"Hello Mrs. Smith. How are you?" she asks. Edith Smith and her husband welcomed Chloe to the floor.

"Other than our new neighbor and the ruckus they are bringing, I am just fine. What about you?" her aging voice asks.

"Great. I am headed for my yearly camp excursion. Can you keep an eye on my place?" Chloe asks.

"Yes dear, I will certainly do that," she agrees.

(Edith and her husband have a spare key to Chloe's apartment.)

"Thank you," Chloe replies as the elevator stops on the main floor.

"You're welcome," she states as Edith exits the car.

Chloe continues to the lower level. As the elevator opens she is met by a repair man. She notices a name tag on his dusty blue shirt. His name is Arnie. "Hello Arnie," she says in passing.

"Hello, Miss," he replies.

The elevator doors close carrying him. Passing several vehicles, she finally reaches her SUV. A short time later, she pulls from the garage and heads toward the camp.

The winding concrete passes beneath her Pathfinder as the city fades and the forest emerges. The fresh air filtering through the trees returns her thoughts to her childhood. She steps off the ocean blue church bus for the first time and is surrounded by strangers. The first person to say hello becomes her best friend.

"Hello, my name is Heather Meager. What is your name?" she loudly asks.

"Hello, I am Chloe Conners," her soft voice answers.

That was the beginning of an inseparable friendship.

That memory causes sadness as she has missed her friend. Chloe decides to telephone her.

"Hello Heather, I am sorry I did not return your call. Can you forgive me?" Chloe begs.

"No!" Heather answers, then hangs up.

Chloe is stunned by the reply. A minute later her phone rings.

"Just kidding, I forgive you! What are you up to?" her friend remarks.

"I deserve that! How are things?" Chloe inquires.

"I am sure you know by now that I am getting divorced and moving home. We must settle the custody arrangement and financial issue.

After that I am returning to Portland! Oh God, I dread the thought of living with my parents once again!" she exhaustingly states.

"Is there anything I can do?" Chloe asks hoping to find redemption.

"Nope, my attorney is dealing with it! So, how have you been?" she inquires.

"Well! I am still engaged but seeing less of each other. Work has put distance between us," Chloe says.

"How is Craig doing?" she asks with fondness echoing in her tone.

"He is fine. The guys went to Seattle this weekend to the Seahawks training camp. I am off on the yearly camp excursion," Chloe offers.

"I do miss the camp. Remember our last year and how you were challenged? That other assistant had your number. What was her name?" Heather remarks.

"Yes, that was the only time my team ever lost!" Chloe states defending her record.

"Good Lord, that loss has really stuck with you!" Heather says baiting her.

"Not at all. I am simply reminding you of all the other wins I have," Chloe says diverting the comment.

"Yeah right. Eight years hasn't been long enough. I remember how you and she became friendly," Heather comments.

"How was that?" Chloe asks.

"She was able to challenge you. You two were similar in the competitive realm," Heather states.

"We we're nothing alike!" Chloe says.

"Yes, you were. The two of you were competitive. The only difference was she got the best of you," Heather states.

"Can we change the subject?" Chloe demands becoming riled.

Heather chuckles knowing her best friend is getting annoyed.

"Okay, what is your role this year?" Heather asks as a smile forms.

"I am a counselor," Chloe says with pride.

"Good for you. You finally get your own cabin," Heather remarks as a chuckle returns.

"Why are you giggling?" Chloe asks as her SUV turns off.

"Because after all these years, you are finally one of the top dogs!" Heather laughs.

"Oh, screw you!" Chloe states.

"I have missed you. I can't wait until I am back home," Heather responds.

"I have missed you as well. I am looking forward to our reunion. Well, I am off to camp! I will call later in the week. Love you, Heather," Chloe states.

"Love you too, Clo!" Heather says.

A smile comes across her fair complexion.

She is greeted by the director and assistants.

"Welcome back, Chloe," Director Erma Hickson says before embracing her protégé.

"Hello Erma. It has been awhile," Chloe states.

"Let me show you to your cabin," Erma states as she pushes her wire-rimmed glasses against her hazel eyes. Erma's short strides increase to match Chloe's. Erma's once brown hair is almost white. Her truly short height is clearly visible as she walks next to Chloe's five - feet-seven-inch height. Erma's round face and sagging chin represent years of loneliness and the joy the camp brings to her. As they approach the cabin, she grunts as her less than long legs lift her up the three stairs. Chloe notices a new cabin next to hers.

"When was that built?" she asks.

"A private donor built that in the spring! They also built a new one for me!" she says with joy.

"Who is the donor?" Chloe inquires.

"Not sure. The money came from a holding company based out of Reno," Erma states.

As Chloe opens the door to her cabin, she is taken by surprise at the cleanliness.

"We have another counselor coming later today. So, take stock of what we may need and the two of you will get the supplies later," Erma says.

Chloe smiles as she is left to settle in. With her clothes neatly folded and placed in drawer, she opens the door and stares out across the lake. Her small feet pound the dirt as she makes her way to the dock. The calm waters barely tease the shore as the waves glide over the sand. She allows the sunshine to drift her back in time.

It is a moonless night and her challenger is standing next to her. Their competitive nature has united them secretly. Their pinkies brush one another as the camp is quiet. It is the second to last night of camp. The challenger has ignited a curiosity in Chloe that she must put out.

"Where do we go from here?" the challenger asks.

"Nowhere! This cannot happen, and we will never contact one another again! Goodnight and have a nice life!" Chloe remarks as she walks away.

The past is carried away by the waves as she awakens.

She is summoned by Erma to join her with the other volunteers. Chloe sighs as the past floats away. She makes her way up the hill and toward Erma.

Laura Pryor

"Yes, Ma'am, what can I do for you?" Chloe politely asks.

"Can you guide the volunteers to their cabins? I will lead the guys to theirs," Erma asks.

"Sure!" Chloe responds as the ladies follow her.

They follow her past the dining hall and onto a narrow path. The scent of pine trees lines the path as the young volunteers follow their leader. Arriving at the cabins, Chloe begins her usual speech.

"Ok everyone, listen up. My name is Chloe and I am a counselor. If you need anything feel free to ask. You will have assistants assigned to you. Please utilize them as well. In each cabin you will find a list of activities. We will schedule them later today. Please familiarize yourself with the list. You will be assigned to your teams tonight. Please enjoy the calm tonight because tomorrow will be hectic. Any questions?" she asks.

The silence answers her question. Chloe leaves them to settle in.

Making her way back to her cabin, Chloe glances to the right to find another memory of her challenger.

It is five days before the end of the season. Chloe is returning to her cabin and she spots her challenger sitting next to a young boy. He is crying, and she is comforting him. The boy's knee was bleeding. Chloe watches as her challenger lifts the young child and carries him down the hill. The boy holds onto her tightly as she staggers down the steep grade.

Chloe meets them at the bottom. Her challenger stops at the sight of Chloe. Placing him on a larger rock, the challenger pauses to rest.

"What happened?" Chloe asks.

"He fell. My team was on a hike and he lost his footing," the assistant remarked.

"Do you need help?" Chloe offers.

"Yes, can you get Erma while I take him to the infirmary?" the assistant asks before lifting him.

"Yes, we will meet you there!" Chloe says before darting down the trail.

With the guide rushing in carrying the young boy, Chloe and Erma are waiting for them. Placing him on the table, her challenger steps back to allow Erma to tend to him. Standing next to Chloe, the assistant's gentle hand rest on Chloe's back. Chloe steps away and allows the once welcome hand to slip off. With a confused look the assistant's brown eyes stares at Chloe. Chloe silently whispers, "Stop it!"

The past evaporates again as the warm breeze awakens Chloe.

As mid-afternoon approaches, Erma knocks on Chloe's cabin. The aroma of pine swirls through the open window as Chloe opens the door.

"Hello, Erma!" Chloe says as she invites her in.

"Good. You have settled in nicely, I see. Can you run a few errands for me?" she asks as her wire-rimmed glasses slip down her button nose.

"Sure, what do you need?" Chloe quickly responds.

"Here is a list and can you pick up your co-counselor at the train station at three sharp?" Erma asks.

"Yes, who am I picking up?" Chloe asks.

Instead of responding, she hurries out.

Noticing the time, Chloe hurries out. The thirty-minute drive will land her at the station a few minutes before three. Chloe, lost in her text messages, does not see her co-counselor emerge.

"Hello, Chloe," the familiar gruff voice speaks.

"Son-of-a-bitch! It is you. Hello Andrea Parker," Chloe remarks as a slight smile shows.

For the first time in eight years she is eye to eye with her challenger. The long stare is the same one Andrea gave her on the first night she challenged Chloe. Andrea stands an inch taller than Chloe. Her hair is now mahogany when it was medium brown with blonde highlights. Chloe immediately notices her beauty. Andrea's long, smooth hair accompanies her fuller breast and tight waist.

"Chloe, you look fantastic!" Andrea remarks.

"Are you ready? We have errands to run," Chloe comments coldly before leading the way.

Andrea smiles at the cold, bitchy tone Chloe is showing.

"Wow, you're still pissed over the loss!" Andrea remarks as they head out.

"Not at all! I do not like surprises!" Chloe declares.

"I thought Erma would have told you," Andrea states as she places her luggage in the back.

The ride from the station to downtown was quiet and awkward for Chloe. Andrea would occasionally glance at her driver.

As they arrive at their first stop, Andrea breaks the silence.

"Wow, it has been what eight years?" she states as they walk into the hardware store.

"Something like that," Chloe responds without looking at Andrea.

Noticing the two of them, the older male clerk offers his assistance.

"Good afternoon ladies, can I assist you with something?" he asks.

"Yes, can you find these things?" Chloe asks as she tears a portion of the list off.

"Yes ma'am. It will take me some time," he states before shuffling off.

"Well, since our conversation is so riveting, I am going to browse!" Andrea comments.

Chloe watches as her tight, faded denim shorts and snug t-shirt step away.

Feeling like a log, Chloe joins her at the paint section.

"What made you come back here?" Chloe states with purpose.

"The past. Just kidding, I was bored!" Andrea responds sharply.

As Andrea removes paint samples, Chloe notices Andrea's burn scar on her hand.

"What happened to your hand?" she inquires.

"An accident," Andrea answers.

"What kind of accident?" Chloe continues the conversation.

The browsing continues to the gardening department. With the sun peeking through the fence, Andrea notices Chloe's ring.

"So, are you married now?" she asks.

"No, just engaged," Chloe answers as she fidgets with her ring.

"So what kind of accident caused the damage?" Chloe asks not letting go of the question.

"The kind that involved a car," Andrea replies in her raspy tone.

"So, who is the lucky person?" Andrea asks as she stops in front of the indoor plants.

"His name is Craig," she answers with a hint of joy.

"Is he a good guy?" Andrea says as she attempts to delve into her life.

"Are you seeing anyone?" Chloe asks with coy.

"Not anymore!" Andrea states as she removes a lucky bamboo plant from the rack.

"Bamboo, huh?" Chloe says with a desire of an explanation for the selection.

"It is a lucky bamboo plant. Who knows, maybe I'll get lucky!" she remarks as their eyes meet.

Chloe removes her glance.

"How long have you been engaged?" Andrea asks handing Chloe the plant.

Andrea's fingertips graze Chloe's as she receives the plant. Chloe stands looking at Andrea as she continues to look at the selection.

"About three months. Sorry, you're not seeing anyone," Chloe says trying to learn more.

"Don't be. She cheated, and I walked away," Andrea says allowing her past some sunlight.

"Here, hold this one also!" Andrea says handing her another bamboo plant.

"Why two?" Chloe wonders.

"Never have too much luck," Andrea remarks.

"Excuse me Miss, I have your order ready at the counter," the clerk interjects.

Chloe thanks him and heads toward the counter.

As Chloe heads out, Andrea remains behind.

"Hello Miss Parker, how are you today?" the clerk asks.

"Fantastic, Harry. The hardware store looks incredible!" she says before exiting.

Chloe watches as Andrea approaches. She notices the scalding mark on her hand and how Andrea favors it.

"So, where to now?" Andrea asks as she places the bag with both plants on the floorboard.

"The party store," she replies.

"I have missed this town. Atlanta just doesn't have the charm that this place has," Andrea says allowing Chloe a little insight.

"You live in Atlanta?" Chloe asks.

"Yes, it has southern charm and history, but the pace wears on a person," Andrea remarks.

"I like to get away every now and then too?" Chloe says as she thinks about her cabin.

"Well, it looks like we're here," Chloe states the obvious as the Pathfinder pulls onto the lot.

"How many more stops?" Andrea asks showing exhaustion.

"One more," Chloe says looking at the list.

"Do you mind if I go with you. I need to stretch my legs after the long train ride?" Andrea says hoping she says yes.

"Suit yourself, but I would appreciate the help," Chloe says gladly accepting Andrea's offer.

With the entrance arriving, Andrea's phone beeps. She opens the message and smiles. Seconds pass before she excuses herself.

"Pardon me, I need to place a call," Andrea says stepping away.

"We were right! Make several copies of this and keep investigating!" she says before pressing the end button.

Her thoughts revert to the day the accident happened. She remembers reaching into the flame, but her memory skips the rest. She forces the past back into hiding as her screen shows her and another young woman smiling together.

Andrea rejoins Chloe by the prize section.

"Can I help with the list?" Andrea asks glancing at Chloe's strong profile.

"Sure, we need to find cheap gifts for prizes," Chloe says.

"You know, I always hated those cheap prizes. What about you?" Andrea says smiling at Chloe.

"They're always awful. I say we buy better ones, if you're willing to go in halves?" Chloe asks not sure of Andrea's financial abilities.

"Sure. So, how do you want to sort the items?" Andrea asks.

"We need bags or boxes," Chloe says thinking out loud.

"One sec!" Andrea says darting toward the register.

She returns with a handful of bags. They separate the bags by age and gender. The bags fill quickly as they reach the final aisle.

"So, what kind of trophy will my team get this year?" Chloe asks knowing a pithy comeback will follow.

"Second place kind!" Andrea declares as they look at prize ribbons. Andrea speaks a question from the past.

"Hey, why did you quit talking to me eight years ago?"

"I told you why on the dock that night!" Chloe says caught off guard.

"No, I mean few days before that?" Andrea asks staring at Chloe.

"We cannot go there," Chloe states as she heads toward the cashier.

"I know, but you were my only other friend. Or at least I thought so," Andrea says with a tear forming.

She passes Chloe tossing a Benjamin Franklin into the cart. Andrea walks to the SUV and waits for Chloe. Chloe notices her head lower as she walks away.

As she arrives, Andrea walks to the back and helps her load the bags. No words are spoken, but a brush of shoulders speaks volumes. Chloe steps away and closes the back after the last bag is loaded.

"Now, where to?" Andrea speaks breaking the silence.

"We have to pick up the t-shirts," Chloe answers with a distant tone as her thoughts hover on Andrea's question.

"I have missed this town. It is nothing like Atlanta. I also miss Portland," Andrea says trying to goat a conversation from Chloe.

"I could not imagine living anywhere else," Chloe finally comments.

"I couldn't either at one time, but life sometimes has other plans," Andrea replies looking at the old building as they pass.

"True!" Chloe answers with one word.

"As much as I have missed Portland, I have missed you and Erma more," Andrea says as the Pathfinder stops at a light.

"That was a long time ago. I have not given that any thought!" Chloe says pulling into a gravel lot.

"I'll run in this time," Andrea says opening the door.

Chloe stares at the brick building fighting the past in her thoughts.

With her long legs, the stairs are conquered quickly. Ten minutes pass, Andrea finally strolls out carrying a large box. She is followed by a young, attractive lady carrying another box. Chloe opens the back as she stands waiting on them.

"Thank you, Stacy!" Andrea says taking the box from her. Andrea leans in and kisses Stacy on the cheek.

"Tell your parent's hello!" Andrea says closing the door.

"I sure will, Andrea!" her young voice replies.

As the SUV exits the lot and heads toward the camp, Andrea grins feeling the coldness of a sharp question coming.

"What was that all about?" Chloe says.

"What was what about?" Andrea replies teasing her.

"That kiss?" Chloe cuts to the point.

"Why are you jealous?" Andrea says knowing Chloe is about to take the bait.

"No, I just think she is awfully young, even for you!" Chloe interjects.

"How do you know what my age preference is? Or do you think I should be with someone more our age? Hey, perhaps I should be with you?" Andrea says compiling the questions.

"There is no *us*!" Chloe exclaims releasing her anger.

"There once was!" Andrea states.

Chloe suddenly pulls to the side of the road. Twisting in her seat, she stares down the brown eyes looking at her

"That was not anything but the escapades of youth. It and you have no meaning to me nor will it ever!" she says yelling at Andrea.

"Okay!" Andrea answers as the SUV returns to the road.

The darkening skies hide the road as they return.

Chapter Six

Chloe and Andrea find themselves in unfamiliar roles as they sit next to one another with a room filled with volunteers and Erma at the activity registration. The twelve volunteers are introduced to Andrea and they begin planning the activities schedule and assigning the volunteers to their groups. Chloe is assigned to counsel groups red and blue. Andrea is assigned to the yellow and green groups.

"Imagine that, I am assigned to the red group!" Chloe antagonistically remarks to Andrea.

"How did that work out last time?" she immediately returns the comment.

Andrea stares at Chloe with her same glare before walking away. "Okay, I am leaving the scheduling to the two of you. So, keep it civil!" Erma instructs them before retiring for the evening.

Each group is divided by age. Groups red and yellow are comprised of ages twelve to eighteen. Groups green and blue are comprised of ages eleven and younger. After the activities are sorted and each group is assigned the appropriate activities, they sit around the campfire.

One of the volunteers inquire about the "keep it civil" comment.

"What was Erma's comment about?" the young man asks.

"Well, let's just say I am extremely competitive and confident person," Chloe adds.

"Yeah, and that is why my team won the last time we were here together," Andrea states.

Andrea takes a spot on the log next to a new volunteer and strikes up a conversation.

"Hi, I'm Andrea!" she says offering her hand.

"Hello, I'm Page. It is nice to meet you," she sweetly says. Page has short, spiky ebony hair. Her long face and square jaw bring a confidence to her aura.

Chloe watches the interaction between the two. As the idol conversations engulf the fire, Chloe occasionally glances at Andrea. The laughter and chatter are stopped as Chloe's phone rings.

"Excuse me. It is my fiancé!" she states before stepping away.

As she steps away, Andrea watches her disappear into the darkness.

Her return is met by two less people. She notices Andrea and Page have left. Chloe is once more in the spotlight when the conversation turns toward her.

"How long have you been engaged?" one of the senior volunteers asks.

"A short time. He is in Seattle this weekend with the guys," she confidently answers.

"Awe, young love is so romantic," a lady named Evelyn comments.

A male volunteer notices Andrea and Page returning.

"Oh, there they are."

Chloe instantly looks at Andrea. They're returning from the trail leading to the cabins. As they close in, Andrea is carrying a bag and Page has the pokers.

"Does anyone want to toast marshmallows?" Page asks.

Page passes the pokers around as the hands rise. Placing her hand on Chloe's shoulder, Andrea offers her the bag of marshmallows. As the evening turns late, the group thins.

"Well, it is getting late, and I am going to turn in. Goodnight everyone. Chloe and Andrea, it is nice to have met such legends!" Page says in a deep, smooth tone.

"Nice to have met you as well," Chloe states.

"Do you remember the shortcut to the cabins?" Andrea asks.

"Yep!" Page confirms.

The once loud group dwindles to a few. Andrea excuses herself as the embers glow. She makes her way to the dock. Knowing Andrea's sexual preference, Chloe wants to confront her about any expectations she might have when it comes to the volunteers. She waits for the rest of the volunteers to retire before doing so. Using her shoe, Chloe racks loose dirt onto the remaining embers. She looks out at the dock at Andrea sitting. As she approaches, Andrea is startled.

"Hello," Andrea says as her stare returns to the black water.

"Hey, why did you take the train? I would have thought driving or flying would have been quicker," Chloe asks trying to remain civil.

"I just wanted to relax and remember things in a quiet moment. I was feeling nostalgic. The alone time provided me with the chance to reflect on the past, and how often it appears," Andrea truthfully states with her knees drawn to her chest.

"I have not given you a second thought. It meant nothing to me then nor now!" Chloe states with the intent on being direct and hurtful.

"I know!" Andrea answers with her throat thickening with emotion and her tender brown eyes tearing.

"Hey, what else did you show her on the trail?" Chloe asks as she leans against the rail.

"What?" Andrea asks with surprise at the question.

"I take this camp very seriously and the excellent reputation it has," Chloe sharply states.

"Chill out and stop being a bitch! You are acting like a jealous teenager!" Andrea says in a raised voice.

"I am not jealous. I have a fiancé. So, keep your actions pure!" Chloe scolds her before leaving.

"What a first! Chloe Conner's walking away!" Andrea states referring to the last time they were on the dock.

"That was a long time ago. So, let's leave it in the past!" Chloe remarks changing her tone as she turns around.

"Apparently not long enough by your reaction to Page and me!" Andrea states as she walks by.

"What does that mean?" Chloe asks as she grabs Andrea's hand.

"Why, this cannot happen! If I remember your last words to me," Andrea say staring at Chloe.

Chloe releases her hand as Andrea pulls away. Chloe watches as the darkness engulfs Andrea.

Returning to her cabin, Andrea hears Chloe's cabin door slam next door. She smiles knowing Chloe still cares. Leaning against the wall, Andrea rests on her bed. Her scarred hand aches as she thinks about the last eight years. She was born and raised in Portland. However, life landed her in Atlanta. She has fought, scraped and crossed boundaries to land where she is now. Today went as planned. Now she will have to contain the onslaught of Chloe's background inquires to come.

In the meantime, Chloe calls Taylor.

"Hey Tay, can you research someone?" Chloe asks.

"Sure, the name is?" Taylor asks as she prepares to write the information down.

"The name is Andrea Parker. She is originally from Portland but now resides in Atlanta. Please be thorough," Chloe instructs.

"Sure will. I will update you when I know something," Taylor responds.

"Goodnight Tay!" Chloe adds.

As the phone call ends, Chloe's long day catches up. She notices a bamboo plant sitting on the table in the corner with a note leaning against the purple foil the pot is wrapped in. Her curiosity lifts her from the bed. Her thin tiring hand opens the note.

Thought you could use a little luck.
Maybe you will win this year.
A

She grins at the jester.

Chapter Seven

Chloe awakens to the beginning of dawn. The smell of pine trees and fresh air renews her spirits. She heads toward the showers. The empty building allows her alone time before the rush of first day happens. As the hot water drops on her blonde hair, Chloe is unaware of an audience approaching. As she turns off the faucet, Andrea and Page walk in.

"Hello, Chloe," Page says as Andrea and Chloe lock eyes.

"Hello, Page," Chloe returns the greeting with droplets landing on her lips.

As she wraps the towel around her, Chloe brushes Andrea's arm as she walks by. Andrea smiles as she slips the towel off and places it across the door.

"Page, which group are you assigned to?" Andrea asks as the hot water drizzles over her well-toned body.

"Blue group, why?" she asks as the water beads on her shoulder.

"Oh good, you got Chloe's group. I was hoping so. Just don't let her run over you. She can be extremely competitive and sometimes that drive can give her tunnel vision," Andrea says.

"That is how you beat her before, isn't it?" Page states.

"That is one of the reasons, but I will not reveal all the tells!" Andrea says as she smiles at Page.

"Fair enough!" Page answers.

They shower quickly after.

Andrea is met by a gentle breeze as she steps onto the tiny patio on her cabin. The quiet of the lake allows her thoughts to drift back to the last day she saw her parents together.

She is alone in a world that has tumbled around her as she steps in front of the white building supported by columns. Each step is met by countless eyes and gossip. Her left arm in a sling and with her hand badly damaged, Andrea takes another step. The blonde streaks in her chestnut hair drape over her sad shoulders. As the top step is reached, her hand grips the brass handle.

Her dreams fade as voices from the trail increase. Andrea re-enters the cabin before anyone notices her. The door closes, and she slides against it with her tears falling. She has fought every moment alone to hide the past. It is easy around others. The night time and alone time allow her guilt to submerge her strength. She recovers shortly and joins the others in the dining hall.

As she walks into the yellow building all eyes are on her, especially Chloe's. She ignores the stares and joins the service line. Erma is watching as Chloe stands beside Andrea.

"Good morning," Chloe offers in a pleasant tone.

"Morning. Are you ready for the first day?" Andrea asks.

"As much as I can be. Are you?" she responds.

"Yep," Andrea says sliding her plate under the window.

"Did you enjoy the hot shower in the new building?" Chloe asks as her plate joins Andrea's.

"Yeah, and how was yours?" Andrea inquires as breakfast is being loaded on her blue plate.

"It was cozy! How was yours?" Chloe asks..

"Lonely," Andrea states as she moves with the line.

"What? The lucky bamboo didn't work?" Chloe quickly reciprocates.

"Not yet," Andrea says looking at Page and then Chloe.

"That was the past," Chloe says in defense.

"Sure, it is," Andrea states as she exits the line.

They sit at different tables.

Mid-morning arrives as well as the rest of the supplies. With the help of the volunteers, the supplies are situated in their designated areas. As Page and Andrea return from taking the swimming supplies to the lake, they are met with a rush of campers.

"Omg, this is crazy!" Page states.

"Just stick next to Chloe as she separates her team. I am going to the opposite side. Later," Andrea speaks.

"Later," she replies.

Page makes her way through the charging children and frolicking teens to find Chloe.

"Okay, Counselor, what do you need from me?" Page asks as she stands next to Chloe.

"Oh good, you're back. Take this list of names and gather your team," Chloe says as she hands her the list.

Page starts at the top and works her way down the list. She hears moans, groans and cheers as the names are called. Slowly the disarray is organized, and the parents disperse. Each group is separated and shown to their cabins. The guys are to the right of the lake and the gals are to the left. As each cabin is assigned, the buddy system is activated. After settling in, the groups are brought back together. They are handed colored shirts based on their team. The red and yellow teams go on a hike first. The blue and green teams are shown their activities. Erma and Page along with three other volunteers introduce the groups to their activities and hand them a map as they tour.

Then Chloe and Andrea introduce themselves to the teams.

"There will be several competitions between our groups. Remember, if you're on the red team, we will win!" Chloe stakes the challenge immediately.

Andrea begins to look around.

"What are you looking for?" Chloe inquires.

"Real competition. Nope, not seeing any for the yellow group," Andrea sarcastically states.

The groups laugh as Chloe grins.

"Seriously, this is a friendly competition and do not make it personal," Andrea remarks as she glances at Chloe.

"Screw that notion. May the best team win!" Chloe response as her tunnel vision kicks in.

The groups begin the hike. Andrea and Chloe follow behind.

The trail begins to wind through the woods. Chloe looks confused.

"Why the confused look?" Andrea asks.

"I do not remember this trail leading toward the woods," she says.

"It has been too long for me. I remember the last day here. After you had left, I walked our trails one last time," Andrea replies.

Andrea is wearing Khaki shorts and a white t-shirt with a peace logo. Her leather sandals glide across the stick-laden path. Chloe is dressed in cut-off denims with a light steel colored tank top with red and white plaid open-collared shirt.

"Why did you do that?" Chloe inquires wanting to hear her words.

"Because, the words you spoke to me on the dock was the last time we were alone. So, I simply wanted to be near you one last time," Andrea honestly answers as she looks at the lake.

"I told you that none of that meant anything to me," Chloe quickly adds as a slight breeze tickles her long ash blonde hair.

"But yet here we are back where it all began," Andrea inserts quickly.

"What did I say yesterday and last night? You and that summer meant nothing to me. So, quit recalling the past. It has no meaning to me!" Chloe angrily reasserts as Andrea glances at the blonde's muscular arms and toned legs.

"I get and hear your words. I know I meant nothing to you, but you do not have the right to tell me where and when I recall things!" Andrea returns the sharp tone.

Their steps continue in silence for several minutes. Chloe begins the conversation once more.

"What, is in Atlanta?" Chloe asks as she watches the group.

"A life I built!" Andrea quickly offers.

"What kind of life did you build?" Chloe asks hoping for a longer conversation.

"One that I had to scrap, fight and accomplish on my own!" Andrea says as her struggles flash in her thoughts.

"That is how you see yourself, huh? As a loner," Chloe states.

"No not anymore, but at one time I was," Andrea rebuffs her comment.

"That is a good thing. Being alone is always hard," Chloe says attempting relate.

"What do you know about being alone?" Andrea aggressively adds.

"I know what being alone with my thoughts and desires are like. I also know what conforming is as well," Chloe returns the question with a statement. "Are you and Page a thing?" Chloe boldly asks.

"Why? Are you jealous?" Andrea returns comment for comment.

"Nope, just making conversation," she replies as her hand brushes Andrea's.

As the group's pace slows, Andrea takes a moment to rest against an old sycamore tree. Chloe begins to speak not realizing Andrea has stopped.

"Oh, sorry. I did not realize you had stopped to rest," Chloe says noticing Andrea resting with her eyes closed.

"I just needed a second. You know why I stopped at this tree?" Andrea asks as images flare in her thoughts.

"No," Chloe rapidly responds.

"Yes, you do! I just thought about the first time." Andrea remarks as Chloe stares at her.

"Just stop. That must stay in the past! I am not the same person!" she says scolding Andrea for the nostalgic moment.

"Yeah, I know. That is what you keep saying. But, yet you keep asking about Page and me," Andrea states as she walks past her.

With frustration building, Chloe quickens her pace as she walks ahead.

Andrea hangs back of the group. Chloe joins the group as they continue hiking. Andrea often looks at her hand as the past is never the past. As the hike turns toward the lake, her phone rings.

"This is Andrea!" she answers.

"The first inquiry from her just came in. The other subject from last night had a late- night guest. How do we proceed?" the male voice asks.

"Good, she is still predictable in her research. Find out who the guest was and make sure they have another late night," Andrea answers.

"Will do. How much does her inquiry learn?" the male voice asks.

"Only of the success. The climb is mine to tell," Andrea instructs him.

"Will keep you apprised of any developments," he says before ending the call.

With phone call ending, a female camper approaches her.

"Hello, my name is Neela and I am on your team," she speaks.

"Hello Neela. It is nice to meet you. Where are you from?" Andrea asks.

"My family originates from Somalia. We came here when I was very young. Are you from Portland?" she asks with an inquisitive tone.

"Originally, yes. I now reside in Atlanta or as it is sometimes referred to as 'Hotlanta'!" Andrea's friendly tone answers.

"What brought you back home?" Neely asks as her light complexion beams off the sun rays on the lake.

"I had some business to attend to. So, I thought it would be wonderful to volunteer again. So, what is your denomination?" Andrea asks.

"None, that is why I am happy to be here. I was so happy to find a camp not based on religion. When I heard this was bought and changed to a camp for all, I was ecstatic!" she says with joy.

"I was surprised it was changed also. I think the new owner was brilliant making this a one-for-all camp," she adds.

"Did you attend when you were younger?" she asks.

"Yes, my first and only time was when my eighteenth birthday was nearing. My family signed me up and I complained all the way here. After the first campfire, I found a friend, and everything was okay," Andrea says. "Sometimes the right things happen when you least expect it!" Andrea adds.

Neely and Andrea stroll along the path talking about life while the rest of the group returns to camp.

The dinner bell rings. Andrea and Neely wash up and join the groups in the hall. Chloe notices Neely's expression of joy. The young lady continues speaking with Andrea. Curiosity creeps up drawing Chloe to join them.

She stands next to Neely.

"Wow, that was a long hike," Chloe says.

"Yes, Chloe, it was. I enjoyed sharing experiences with Andrea," Neely says as her plate slides under the partition.

"Did you know she is originally from Somalia? Her family came to Portland when she was young," Andrea remarks.

"No, I did not. What an amazing story!" Chloe says.

"I told Andrea how happy I am to find a camp not based on religion," Neely remarks.

"Yes, this use to be a church-based camp. The new owners found changing the name and criteria to 'All are welcome' has increased popularity and revenue," Chloe adds.

"Is the attendance higher than before?" Andrea inquires.

"Yes, the last three years has seen a steady increase in attendance. I noticed the cabins and showers are all new," Chloe adds.

"Thank God. This was really worn the last time I was here," Andrea comments.

As Neely removes her tray from the counter, she joins her friends at another table.

Andrea shakes her head as the mashed potatoes are slopped on her tray. "Well maybe the food still needs some work!" she comments sliding her tray to the next station.

Chloe smiles and exits the line. She joins Erma.

"Hello, how is the day going?" Chloe asks.

"Well, besides the normal tummy aches, whining and crying, everything is good," Erma remarks as she butters her roll.

"Who are the new owners?" Chloe asks as she spoons the gravy from her chicken.

"All I know is they're based out of Reno. They have spent a lot of money upgrading most things. My paycheck is steady," Erma says between bites.

"What are the two of you discussing?" Andrea asks as she sits next to Chloe.

"We're talking about the upgrades the new owners have made," Erma says.

"I cannot believe the cabins and shower. That was a must!" Andrea remarks.

"I wonder who they are?" Chloe asks.

"Does it matter as long as the place is profitable?" Andrea states.

"Not to my paycheck!" Erma response as a chuckle crosses her round face.

"How was the first day for the two of you?" Erma asks as her potatoes become limp.

"It was hectic at first, but for the most part everything went well," Andrea says as her foot touches Chloe's.

"When did the trail change?" Chloe inquires slipping her foot away.

"The new owners bought the surrounding property and expanded the trails last spring." Erma answers.

"I think they did an amazing job," Andrea states.

"Are we going to have another campfire tonight?" Andrea asks.

"Yes, after the younger groups are tucked in," Erma says.

"Good!" Andrea states.

"Hey, maybe you can wonder off again," Chloe says with a smirk.

"Hey, maybe your fiancé can call again!" Andrea returns the comment.

"Knock it off, you two. I swear, eight years has not been long enough!" Erma admonishes them.

"Deal!" Andrea states as she excuses herself.

As Andrea leaves the hall and walks to her cabin, Chloe and Erma continue their conversation.

"Why did she return after all these years?" Chloe asks referring to Andrea.

"She called me up a month ago and volunteered to be a counselor. I know what you are thinking. We have been in contact through the years. So, stop the judging. Andrea has been through a lot," Erma states.

"Who hasn't?" Chloe says.

"More than her share! Her life has been a struggle and she climbed out of hell! So, climb down from your high-horse!" Erma says.

Her words settle into Chloe's tone as the conversation changes.

The dinner ends, and the evening activities begin. For the blue and green groups, they learn about the stars. Page and the other volunteers teach them about the Big Dipper and the North Star. As Page points to the sky, Andrea joins them.

"Have any of you heard of the Greek gods?" Andrea asks.

With several hands raised, she asks them to tell what they have learned. Andrea sits on the ground next to them listening to their stories. Page is sitting across from Andrea.

How many of you have just laid back and watched the stars shine? Andrea asks in a light-hearted tone.

One of the children raise their hand and Andrea takes the cue.

"Well, why don't we show everyone how to," Page says as she lays back.

The group looked like dominoes as they fell back. Leaning against the dock, Chloe watches Andrea interact with the youngster and Page. As the rest of the groups notice the youngster, they seem to take an interest in their activity. Chloe watches as some of the teenagers do the same.

"Wow, I have not done this for years," one of the young lady's comment.

Chloe lowers the volume on the radio and allows the peace to creep into her thoughts as she leans against the rail. Her blue eyes close as eight years melt away.

It is toward the end of first week of summer camp and she has been having weird feelings weaving through her mind. She hears a splash from behind. In a sudden turn, she watches Andrea swim. She steps back into the woods and intently stares as Andrea emerges from the water. She struggles to deny her inquisitive notions. As Andrea passes, Chloe remains frozen in thought. Andrea's well-formed figure has Chloe ashamed of her flatness. Andrea suddenly stops, and Chloe catches her breath. With a grin reaching each ear, Andrea turns. Each step sinks into the dirt, as she approaches Chloe. Chloe's blue eyes widen as Andrea reaches for her. Andrea's damp hands push Chloe further into the thickets as Chloe's back bumps the sycamore tree. Her movement stops and Andrea stares into her nervous deep blue eyes. Andrea's long fingers brush Chloe's light blonde hair away from her tan complexion. As noise from a close trail interrupts the stare, Andrea moves in closer. Chloe is unable to move for fear of being seen. When Chloe looks to the trail, Andrea places her hand on Chloe's cool cheek and turns her head to face her.

Andrea steps into Chloe and whispers "Quiet!"

Chloe nervously glares into Andrea's soft brown eyes. Andrea smiles before placing her lips against Chloe's. As the moonlight peeks through the clouds, Andrea's skin glows as the water drips on Chloe's skin. The kiss ends and Andrea stares into Chloe's eyes. She waits for the trail to grow quiet before walking away. Her dreaming ends as the wind blows.

Chloe allows the dream to float away as she rejoins her group. Evening ends for the children as Andrea and Page escort them to their bunks. As the two male volunteers prepare the campfire, Andrea and Page stroll along the trail heading back to the campfire. Chloe watches with intent as they emerge. She fake smiles at them sensing Andrea is attracted to Page. Chloe understands the past and knows it has no meaning in the present. She strikes up conversation with other guides and volunteers. The inevitable happens as the ghost stories begin. One after another until it is Andrea's turn. She slides down the log and rests her back against it. Her expression grows dark as she begins.

"It was a winter night many years ago. Two teenagers were driving home from a party they were told not to attend. The coastline was hauntingly dark as the moon was shielded by the oncoming storm clouds. The older sister was speeding trying to beat their curfew. It happened so quickly. A strange figure stepped from the tree line and she overreacted turning the wheel. The damp road took control of the car and twisted it against the guard rail. As the driver awoke, a strong odor of gasoline filled the air. She saw the can fall to the pavement as a hand with a lighted match reached into the car. The fumes were ignited as the driver panicked to save her sister. The hand with the match disappeared as the driver reached into the car to free her sister from the seatbelt. The flames spiked and scalded her hand as her attempt became futile. The driver screamed in pain while her hand burned. Her eyes glance over the car at the tree line as the figure watched the car burn. Now I must live with scar of that damn accident. I avoid the coastline for fear of the figure. There have been reports over the years about someone standing in the tree line."

Andrea rubs her hand as the story ends. Andrea smiles as looks of fear resonate through the flames.

"Just a story. I burned my hand attempting to cook," she chuckles as the mood lightens.

"On that note, I am going to stretch my legs," Andrea states as she glances at Chloe.

Chloe notices a flinch from Page as Andrea stands.

"Oh Andrea, by the way, I noticed a scheduling issue I need to show you before tomorrow. Sorry, I just remembered it," Chloe says as she dusts her bottom off.

"Sure, I'll meet you in the canteen in a few," Andrea agrees. As she walks away, Chloe heads in the opposite direction.

As she reaches her cabin, Chloe notices a message on the phone.

"Clo, I am unable to find anything about Andrea Parker from Atlanta. I will keep searching," Taylor texts.

Deleting the text, Chloe retrieves the schedule from the corkboard on the wall. She walks quickly to meet Andrea. The screen door shrieks. She closes it behind her.

"Andrea, where are you?" she loudly asks.

"In the back."

Chloe walks around the counter and into the supply room.

"Hey, what problem is there?" Andrea asks.

"What are you putting on your hand?" Chloe asks as Andrea rubs a cream in her scarred skin.

"It is a pain cream that eases the nerve damage and softens the skin. Well, softens as much as possible. Why?" Andrea asks as she glances at Chloe.

"Does it hurt a lot?" Chloe asks as she reaches for her hand.

"Some days more than others. Can you hand me a paper towel?" Andrea pleads as Chloe's touch ignites a beat in her heart.

"May I help you?" Chloe asks as she hands Andrea the towel.

Andrea replies by offering her right hand to her to wipe the cream off. Andrea's subtle gentle wanting eyes draw Chloe's stare.

"Your hair is darker and longer than before," Chloe comments as she slowly wipes the cream off.

"Your hair is lighter and a little shorter. It looks nice on you," Andrea says wanting to converse.

"Has Portland changed a lot?" Andrea asks.

"Some. How is Megan?" Chloe asks the one question Andrea cannot hide from.

"She died almost eight years ago," Andrea answers with shame.

Seeing her pain, Chloe feels helpless.

"I am sorry! I did not know!" Chloe states watching the anguish in Andrea's brown eyes.

"It's okay. It was a long time ago, even though her image is always fresh in my dreams." Andrea answers without any walls.

Their words dance around the thoughts echoing in their minds.

"So how long have you lived in Atlanta?" Chloe inquires as she holds Andrea's hand.

"Eight years next July. Have you ever thought about us?" Andrea bluntly asks.

"*Us* no, but *you* yes. There really is no *us*!" Chloe states as she tosses the towel into the trash.

The moment of silence packs the small room as they look at one another. Andrea prepares to speak but is interrupted by the closing of the screen door.

"Andrea are you in here?" Page's voice asks.

"Yes, we're back here," Andrea replies.

"Oh, I did not know you were in here, Chloe. Are you returning to the campfire?" she asks.

"Yeah, give me a sec," Andrea answers.

"No biggie, we can talk about the scheduling issue first thing," Chloe states before stepping out.

Andrea watches as Chloe walks away. Chloe retires to her cabin for the evening.

Chapter Eight

The next morning finds daybreak peaking over the camp. Chloe is on the last leg of her morning run as she spots Page coming out of Andrea's cabin. She paces the trail passing Andrea standing in the doorway. Without a glance, Chloe races inside. She quickly grabs her towel and bag before heading for the showers. Andrea smiles at her as she leaves the cabin.

Chloe's steadfast focus does not entertain Andrea's gesture. Andrea follows Chloe. The hot water steams the cubicle. As Chloe hangs her towel over the partition, Andrea stomps in.

"Hey, what was that all about?" she demands as Chloe lowers her head under the water.

"What was what all about?" Chloe asks as she squeezes a dab of shampoo in her palm.

"Not looking at me or waving back? I thought we were past that last night?" Andrea sharply demands.

"Sorry, just focused on getting my things and beating the crowd to the showers," Chloe states as she continues to shower.

Chloe ignores Andrea's dark stare. She finishes and steps out. As Chloe grabs her bag, Andrea reaches for her arm. Chloe quickly snatches the bag from the shelf and heads toward the dressing room. In a hurrying state, Chloe drops the towel wrapped around her after entering the room. Andrea marches in as Chloe slips her denim shorts on. (Andrea pauses briefly to appreciate Chloe's figure. Then continues.) She steps up to Chloe as she pulls her t-shirt over her breast. Chloe is surprised to find Andrea standing inches from her.

"Excuse me, I will be out of the way shortly," Chloe remarks as Andrea chest is touching hers.

Andrea pushes Chloe against the mirror. Andrea attempts to place her arms around Chloe. Chloe steps around the attempt and accidently smashes Andrea's damaged hand against the wall.

"Ouch!" Andrea says grimacing in pain as she favors her hand.

Andrea's scream turns Chloe's attention toward her.

"I'm sorry!" Chloe says before walking away.

The dining hall was loud. The coldness between Andrea and Chloe could freeze the lake. The groups are separated by their colors and Chloe gathers her teams.

"Can I have everyone's attention? I need the red team to meet at the archery section. The blue team needs to meet at the dock. Red team, you are first at archery. Blue team, you are going to learn how to canoe. Any questions?" Chloe states.

"Wait a minute, the yellow team was first at archery," Andrea says as she steps through the red team.

"Not anymore, I tried to explain to you last night about the scheduling issue and we were interrupted. So, I claimed it first. Your team can practice tetherball! Let's go team. We have a challenge to prepare for!" Chloe arrogantly says.

Erma stands back and watches the events unfold as she thinks to herself, *Here, we go. So much for civility.*

Andrea sprints to catch up with Chloe.

She disrupts Chloe's path by stepping in front of her.

"So, this is how it is going to be? Eight years all over again?" Andrea states looking into Chloe's strong demeanor and touching her forearm.

"Nope, I will win this time! What's wrong, late night?" Chloe asks as she refers to Page leaving her cabin.

Andrea is speechless as Chloe steps around her. In walking back to her group, Andrea's anger subsides.

"Okay team, we lost this battle. Believe me, we are at war and we will win. Are you with me? Are we going to win the entire challenge?" she asks her groups.

In unity they answer, "YES!"

"Good, we will keep it clean and fair. Now let us practice and excel!" Andrea says.

Andrea stares at Chloe as revenge suffocates her thoughts.

"Andrea, how are we going to disrupt their routines?" the yellow team guide inquires.

"We're not. I am! I do not want the teams involved. I only want them to have fun and enjoy themselves. If you hear any of them plotting or talking about doing something, let me know," Andrea instructs.

"Will do," the guide says as she rejoins her team.

Andrea stands alone with the lake at her back. Chloe notices Andrea's glare as she instructs the team.

"Yeah, you just go ahead and try to pull the same snobbish shit as last time. We'll see where it gets you!" Andrea says to herself.

While Chloe basks in her momentary win, Andrea sneaks off. Her hand slowly opens her competitor's door. Her search does not take long as she grins.

The sun sets across the lake and the songs begin. The evening events are for all ages. One of the events is dancing. As the children hop and jump around in what can be called dancing, the other groups dance with them. Page watches the tension between Andrea and Chloe.

"So, are you going to talk to her?" Page asks Andrea.

"Nope, she can come to me," Andrea replies.

"The two of you do realize this is affecting the entire camp, right?" she comments in a scolding manner.

"How is that?" Andrea blindly inquires.

"Because the two of you are acting like toddlers. You should just get it on or we will all need butter knives to cut the air!" Page disciplines her.

Andrea allows her advice to reach her thoughts but does not respond. Page rejoins the children as they laugh and dance.

The singing and dancing continue into the ten o'clock hour. As Chloe notices the time, she starts to wrap up the evening.

"Okay, everyone, it is time to wrap things up!"

The guides gather their groups and escort them to their cabins. The teens are permitted to stay up until eleven. They gather around the beach to share one thing about themselves. This was always Chloe's favorite event. She loved to talk about herself. This time was no different.

"Hello everyone. With exception of my college years, I have come here every summer," Chloe says as the wave brushes her ankles.

Andrea watches Chloe as she shines in the spotlight once more. Andrea takes a seat on the steps leading to her cabin. She allows her fantasies to arrive. The moonless night concealed the first time she held Chloe's nervous hand. Andrea had known her sexuality from a young age. She did conceal it from her parents well into her sophomore year. As par for the course, her life changed when she came out. They were angry and disappointed. Her mother, Allison, had dreams for Andrea. She wanted a large wedding for her. Her father wanted a son-in-law he could hunt with. Andrea's sister, Megan, did not have that opportunity. From the moment Andrea came out, her parent's attention faded. She learned to figure things out on her own. The first day she met Chloe was the moment Andrea knew desire.

As they slipped away from the group, their hearts pounded with anticipation. Chloe joined her at the end of trail five. This was the least used trail due to the hazards. Chloe stood next to Andrea. Their pinkies graze each other as they stood looking at the lake. The waves splashed the rocks below, and their hands intertwined. Chloe's hand shook as Andrea gripped it. With no words needed, the grip spoke volumes.

The remembering is halted by a shadow to her left.

"May I have a seat?" Erma asks as her tone firms.

"Sure," Andrea says.

"So how is this feud going to end this time?" Erma's cracking voice asks.

"With her winning and me leaving next Friday," Andrea speaks with surrender.

"So, you're just going to walk away from a second chance?" Erma remarks with disappointment.

"I have played this game far too long. I will finish any business and head home. At least in Atlanta, the bullshit is business and not personal," Andrea states.

"You have invested all of this time and energy into the last eight years. Why not see things through?" Erma asks as she watches Chloe interact with the teens.

"Because I am exhausted and the thought of chasing the dream for another day longer tires me," Andrea states as she closes her eyes.

"Very well, but you have to tell everyone. I will not!" Erma sternly says.

"Deal," Andrea answers before opening her eyes.

Chloe watches as Erma hugs Andrea. Andrea wipes a tear away before heading inside.

With the evening ending, Chloe ensures the canteen is secured. As she steps away, she is met by Craig. He grabs her by the waist and kisses her. She steps back shocked by his presence.

"What are you doing here?" she asks with an almost angry tone.

"Just wanted to surprise you and tuck you in!" he states with a devilish grin.

"Oh, come on," she says before taking his hand.

Chloe escorts him to her cabin where he spends the night.

Chapter Nine

With the dew resting atop the grass, Chloe is returning to her cabin after escorting him out. Chloe notices Andrea sitting against the rail on the dock. With her knees bent, Andrea looks at Chloe. Chloe realizes Andrea saw Craig leaving her cabin. They stare briefly. Andrea walks in the opposite direction. Chloe returns to her cabin retrieving a towel. Her routine concludes with her stopping at the cabin. As she chooses her shoe selection, Chloe becomes pissed.

"That Bitch!" she remarks walking to Andrea's cabin. Chloe knocks to an empty response. She opens the door and her competitive nature kicks in as she removes the item from the table. With her edginess in high gear, Chloe swings the door open to the dining hall. The room becomes slight as the screen slams behind her. Chloe beelines toward Andrea who is sitting next to Erma. Erma notices the fire in her eyes and knows Andrea is the cause.

"Where are they?" Chloe says slamming her hand on the table in front of Andrea.

"Where's what?" Andrea says being coy.

"I want them back and you're not getting this until I do!" Chloe declares holding the hand cream.

"Give that back!" Andrea loudly asks as she stands to confront Chloe.

Chloe stares briefly before stomping off and out the door.

"You B!" Andrea incompletes the word as she jumps over the table running after Chloe.

"Omg, this is not going to end well!" Erma shouts grabbing Page as she gives chase.

They are face to face screaming at each other when Erma and Page arrive. The dining hall clears to watch the show.

"God damn it, give it to me!" Andrea says shoving Chloe.

"Give them back!" Chloe says returning the shove.

"You're a snobbish, self-centered bitch!" Andrea says pushing her.

"You're a coward!" Chloe says shoving Andrea to the ground.

Andrea springs to her feet and darts toward Chloe. Page intercepts the dart by wrapping her arms around Andrea. With Andrea in hand, Erma yanks on Chloe's ear. They drag them both into her office. The slamming of the office door rattles the room.

"Sit down and shut up! I will not have this ever again. Now what the hell is going on? Erma loudly demands. They both begin to argue. "Stop it! Chloe what are you missing?" Erma shouts.

"My shoelaces!" Chloe says staring at Andrea.

"A pair of shoelaces?" Erma asks with disbelief at the cause of the squabble.

"No not a pair, but all of them are missing!" she says shooting Andrea a glare.

"Andrea, where the hell are the laces?" Erma asks knowing Andrea is guilty.

"I do not have them!" Andrea deflects the question.

"Where did you put them?" Erma restructures her question knowing how Andrea plays word games.

"I did not put them anywhere?" Andrea denies.

"ANDREA, quit with your damn word games and return them to her within the hour. And you, give her the hand cream back!" Erma states losing her temper.

"No, not until the laces are in my hand!" Chloe says stomping out.

Chloe slams the door and Erma returns her focus to Andrea.

"Nice, so tell me how your plan is working? The two of you are going to apologize to the rest of the camp before the hour is up!" Erma says before leaving.

"That smirk better disappear. You have managed to scare the children, piss Erma off and embarrass yourself! But hey, on the bright side, you have Chloe's attention!" Page says waiting for Andrea to leave.

They return to their cabins to stew on the argument for the better part of the hour.

The anger subsides as Andrea gives in to Erma's timeline. She knocks on Chloe's door.

"Hey, can I have my hand cream?" Andrea asks in a mellow tone.

"Hey, can I have my laces?" Chloe asks.

"If I can have my shoes?" Andrea says walking past Chloe.

Chloe watches as Andrea grabs the shoes lined along the wall. With her shoes in hand, Andrea tells her to follow. Andrea opens her cabin door and points to the corner behind the door. Chloe's eyes soften at the sight of her shoes and laces fully intact. Andrea leans against the counter watching Chloe retrieve her shoes.

"Why did you do this?" Chloe asks wanting to know the reason.

"Because you hurt me in the shower. But mostly because I want you to talk to me," Andrea explains.

Chloe walks toward the door. She stops in the entryway in front of Andrea. With her right hand, Chloe places the hand cream in Andrea's right hand.

"Please, Chloe, just talk to me?" Andrea begs holding her hand.

"I can't do this!" Chloe says releasing her hand.

When the group is gathered, they both apologize.

The next five days are competitive with each team winning different events. As Friday arrives, so does the final competition. It is time to capture the opponent's flag.

"Okay, red team, let's capture their flag and wrap up the title!" Chloe shouts.

As the yellow team is gathered, Andrea prepares her speech. She tells the yellow team to persevere and take the flag. "Remember what I taught you about focus and how too much focus can cause tunnel vision. So, do what you can and bring the flag home!"

Erma blows a whistle to signal the gathering of the teams. "Alright, are the teams ready? I hope so! But before we start, Andrea has something to say!" Erma states.

With a deep breath, Andrea steps forward.

"Hello everyone, hope you all have had a great time. I hope you will return to compete next year or you will volunteer. It is always good to repay the joy you have earned. So, on that note, I must tell you I am leaving soon after the yellow team wins! So, let's go and have fun!"

Chloe notices the exhaustion in Andrea's eyes. As the teams separate and take to the woods, Chloe walks up to Andrea.

"So, why are you leaving a day early?" she asks wanting to touch her.

"Because desire and dreams do not always come true. The competing gets old. I came back for you, but it is a little too late," Andrea comments before turning to leave.

Chloe reaches for her tan arm. Her touch draws a passionate stare from Andrea before she walks away. Chloe becomes emotional as her teary eyes share Andrea's feelings.

The competition is in full swing as Andrea leans against their tree. As the breeze dances with the leaves, she thinks about the last eight years. She has acquired bountiful knowledge and contacts through her young twenty-six years. With all the struggles and success, she has never forgot the camp. As the red group shouts victory, Andrea smiles. In the middle of the night, she removed the red team's flag. Yes, she sabotaged her team, but now Chloe can claim victory eight years later. Chloe is hopping and dancing with her team as she waves the flag. Thinking she can slip by unnoticed, Andrea walks away.

As she enters her cabin, her team has left a goodbye card for her. It is on the table. The entire staff and teams have signed it. As she reads the well wishes, her tears begin to stream. She smiles with joy and happiness. Her tears dry, and Andrea removes an envelope from her bag. It is addressed to Erma.

My dear friend and caretaker, thank you for being here for me when my life crashed. Thank you for picking me up and showing me the way. (Three years ago, Erma became ill and was unable to make the payments to the bank. The camp nearly fell into foreclosure. Andrea purchased the camp and restored it. Erma had no idea who purchased it. All she was told it was under new ownership and they're going to do major updates.) Please accept this deed as repayment for all you have done for the young!

Love,
Andrea

As she closes the door behind herself. Andrea walks into Chloe.

"Hey, I am glad you came back," Chloe states touching her arm.

"Hey, me too. It was really nice being back here," Andrea humbly states.

"Craig and I set a wedding date. It will be in November," Chloe says.

"That's good. You need to know the morning you saw Page leaving my cabin was not as it appeared. She came by for a spare towel. There was never anything between us. You were the one I will always desire. But now things must be as they are. So, take care Chloe and be happy," Andrea speaks.

Chloe is stunned by her words. She can only watch her first love walk away. Andrea stops at the fence where Erma is waiting. They hug.

"Erma, please take this and do not open until I am in the cab and pulling away," Andrea states as she releases her.

She glances at Chloe staring at her. Andrea walks to the cab and leaves.

She waits for the cab to drive off before following her instructions. She is dumbfounded upon opening the envelope. As the words and deed sink in, she marches toward Chloe.

"We need to speak!" Erma strongly demands.

"Sure," Chloe answers.

Following her to the office, Erma closes the door behind Chloe.

"Now, to settle something once and for all. You need to know about Andrea. Six months after the two of you left here, Andrea's life changed forever. She was returning from a party with her sister when a deer ran out in front of her. She lost control of the car. The car hit an embankment and caught fire. She burned her hand while trying to save Megan. She sat alone as the rescuer tried to save Megan. She died from her injuries. Her parents blamed Andrea for taking Megan to the party. They disowned her. She had to attend her sister's funeral alone. She was treated as an outcast. They tossed her backpack filled with belongings to the curb and Andrea had nowhere to go. She was left with only a change of clothes and nothing else but loneliness. So, she ended up here, where she was able to finish high school. She went to college in Atlanta. The only reason she returned was for you! That is love and loyalty! So, think about that as you return to your perfect world. I love you, Chloe, but damn it sometimes you can be so self-absorbed!" Erma scolds her.

Chloe is left speechless and sad.

The next day ends Summer Camp. Chloe says goodbye to her friends and Erma before driving off. As she leaves, her phone rings.

"Hello Taylor, what did you find out?"

"The story checks outs. There is a package that arrived yesterday. You may want to open it," Taylor comments.

"Okay, I will stop by on the way home," Chloe says.

Her drive home is filled with the reunion and seeing her secret desire again. All she can think about is how beautiful Andrea was and how she could never tell her so. As she drives home, her phone rings.

"Chloe speaking!"

"Did you win the flag!" Heather asks.

"Yeah!" Chloe answers in a gloomy tone.

"What's wrong? I thought winning was everything?" Heather asks.

"It was, but I did not realize the cost," Chloe answers with clarity.

"So, what is this I hear about Craig and you setting a date?" Heather inquires.

"Yep, it is fifteenth of November. Mom is going to love that," Chloe replies.

"Well, congrats. I am coming home in October, so we can plan away!" Heather says trying to lighten the mood.

"Thank you. I have really missed you. It is going to be great seeing you again," Chloe says as she enters the city.

"Well, my kids are home, so I have to be going," Heather states.

"Love you, Heather," Chloe says.

"Love you, Clo," Heather returns the endearment.

Their conversation ends with Chloe stopping at the firm. She parks on the street and darts inside. The still of the office is a welcome sound from the norm. She enjoys the silence.

An hour later she leaves carrying the package and several files. She makes her normal stop and soon after she is home. Her apartment is a welcome sight. With her shoes chucked off onto the mat, Chloe lays on the sofa. As her twilight nap deepens the doorbell rings. She opens the door to Craig smiling.

"Hello, I lost my key in Seattle," he says walking past her after they smooch. "So, what do you want to do today?" he asks with full energy.

"Nothing. I just want to stay home a relax," she answers.

"Nope, we need to tell family and friends about the wedding! So, get up and let's celebrate!" he urges.

Chloe places her files in the briefcase. They spend the rest of day making the notifications. Their Sunday is spent snuggling and watching old movies. Her mind pretends Andrea is the one holding her.

Chapter Ten

Chloe plays catch up with her clients on Monday. As the seven o'clock hour arrives, so does her exhaustion. The black limousine stops in front of her apartment building. Moments later, the woman enters.

"Has she opened the file?" the voice asks.

"Don't believe so. They were cuddly Saturday night. Sunday, they stayed in. Are you sure this is what you want to do?" he asks.

"Yes, Mr. Tine, I am sure. We have awakened her, now it is time to unravel her!" the voice remarks.

"Have you given any thought as to how she will react?" the female asks.

"Yes, it will be sheer delight seeing her panic," the voice answers.

"Mr. Tine, please have Mr. Griffin inform her tomorrow that his client strongly desires the takeover and will not tolerate obstacles," the voice states.

"For you, my friend, I want everything you can dig up on the mayor," the voice instructs.

"Are you sure, after all he is?" the female reminds her friend.

"That is precisely why!" the voice commands. "Is the apartment ready?" the voice asks.

"Yes," Mr. Tine answers.

"Very good. I will move in tomorrow!" the voice says.

The window rises as the limousine drives away.

Chloe prepares for her ten o'clock standing appointment. She opens her briefcase and places the file in front of her. Her thoughts are about Andrea and what she has been through. She drifts back in time when they shared their first time together. Chloe was frightened, unsure of what to do. Andrea guided Chloe's narrow fingers across her bare chest. Their lips ignited a rush of desire. Andrea lowered herself. A release of desire and curiosity exudes with Chloe's moan. She is awakened by a touch of the shoulder.

"Hey, Chloe, your ten o'clock is here," Taylor says.

"Thank you, Tay," Chloe responds.

She gathers her wandering thoughts. Chloe greets Mr. Griffin at the waiting area and escorts him to her office.

"Please have a seat," she says walking around to her chair.

"So, what have you found out?" he bluntly asks.

"It appears the city council does not want the area to lose a locally owned landmark. They consider your company as an outsider. Therefore, they're going to block the sale, or shall I say take-over, of the business," Chloe states.

"What if we give them some assurances?" he asks sitting with perfect posture.

"What kind of assurances?" she asks leaning forward.

"Well, we would keep most of the staff and hire locally only," he answers looking at the picture on the desk behind her.

"What about remodeling and how that would affect the historical value?" she inquires noticing his wondering eye. "I notice you're looking around me?" she asks as her blue eyes meet his hazel eyes.

"Yes, so sorry! I could not help but notice the picture behind you. Is that your mother and sisters?" he asks.

"Oh no, sir!" she answers before her leather swivel chair spins around. "This is a picture of my last summer camp as a teenager when I was a guide. This is Erma. She is the director. These two are Heather and Andrea. They were fellow guides that summer," Chloe says as she glances at the photograph with fondness.

"It must have been memorable summer?" he asks.

"Yes, more than anyone would realize. Now back to business," she says changing the subject.

"As for remodeling, there are some structural updates along with city ordinances that have to be met. My client is originally from Portland and values the historical significance of Pop's Diner," he adds.

"Where does your client presently reside?" she asks hoping for some insight.

"Right now, about ten-thousand feet above the Midwest. Tomorrow is another story," he says keeping vagueness in the forefront. "The current owners are not willing to sell, and the place is in a deplorable state. My client is not happy about it. So, I want you to encourage the owner to sell to my client. My client will keep their promise to do right by their word," he calmly states.

"I will update you next Tuesday," she states as the meeting ends.

"Very well, Miss Conners, or shall I say soon to be Mrs. Jenkins," he states as his perfect posture walks toward the door. Her puzzled look prompted an explanation of his statement. "Gossip from the waiting area," he says as she walks him out.

"Of course," she says with a slight grin.

As the rest of the morning passes quickly, Chloe finds solitude from the busy morning as the appointments end. She asks Taylor to come in.

"Yes, Chloe, what do you need?" Taylor asks before the clock ticks on the five o'clock hour.

"Can you set up a meeting with the mayor for the end of the week or Monday? When was the last time you went to Pop's Diner?"

"I will try to set a meeting before leaving. As for Pop's, good lord, it has been years. Why?" Taylor asks as she leans against Chloe's desk.

"Are you free for a bit tonight?" Chloe asks as she changes in her bathroom.

"How long is a bit? I have a late dinner date," Taylor inquires.

"Maybe an hour or so," Chloe says as she emerges from her bathroom with her suit neatly folded.

"Wow, that's a different look," Taylor remarks as Chloe ties her running shoes. Chloe is wearing dark denims with a white t-shirt and running shoes.

"Yep. Decided to go casual for a bit. Are you ready?" she asks.

"One sec, let me make the appointment," Taylor states as she walks out.

Chloe locks her briefcase in the safe under her desk and meets Taylor at her desk. As Taylor is confirming the meeting time, Chloe tucks her blonde hair through the Trail Blazers black and red cap.

"Wow, now that is really dressed down. You know Craig would not approve of the hat," Taylor reminds her.

"Yeah, but I can do and wear what I want," Chloe says showing her independence.

"Okay! Your appointment is at three-thirty-five on Friday with the mayor," Taylor says as she walks out ahead of her boss.

"Really, three-thirty- five? Why not three-thirty?" Chloe asks as they signal for a cab.

"The mayor is already dismissing you by the odd appointment. He is hoping you'll be a minute late and then he can refuse to meet with you. It is a secretarial trick. I do it sometimes, when I know you do not have time to meet someone," Taylor says as they stroll pass the shops.

"Where are we going?" Taylor asks.

"I want to check out the condition of the diner for myself. I believe my client's representative, but I need to verify it," Chloe states.

"How was camp? Did you finally win?" Taylor asks as she presses the walk button for the crosswalk.

"Yep, my team finally won. I was so proud of them! It was nice to see Erma again. I need to stay in contact more often," Chloe remarks with a regretful tone.

"You should. So, why are we walking the eight blocks instead of taking a cab?" Taylor asks as her heels pound the concrete.

"Damn, I guess I should have told you about the walk," Chloe says as she watches Taylor grimace in pain.

"It's okay," Taylor remarks.

"Stop, no it is not," Chloe says as she waves for a cab.

"What are you doing?" Taylor asks.

"Getting a cab," Chloe declares.

The cab stops at the curb and Chloe opens the door. Taylor steps in and slides over. Chloe hands Taylor two twenties.

"Aren't you getting in?" Taylor asks as she receives the money.

"Nope. I want to walk. Besides you have a date to prepare for," Chloe says as she steps away.

"See you tomorrow," Taylor comments as the cab pulls away.

Her journey continues block after block. She turns off Southwest Broadway and onto West Burnside Street. The diner is on the corner. She immediately notices the rusted awning and faded sign. The once well-lit name is dark. She opens the cracked but taped glass door and walks in. The once welcoming neighborhood diner is now a depressed, outdated greasy spoon. The smell of old grease permeates the air. She notices dead bugs laying sporadically near the counter. Her skin crawls as a cockroach crawls in front of her. Chloe walks to the counter and asks for the manager. The waitress steps away and disappears through the food stained swing door. While waiting, she turns to look around. The diner's vinyl booths are ripped and torn.

The once white table tops are yellow-stained from years of neglect.

"Excuse me, Miss. I am Ernesto, the manager and owner. How can I help you?" the elderly man says.

"Hello, can we speak in private?" Chloe asks.

He gestures to the back booth with his wrinkled hand and leads the way. He waits for her to sit first.

"Hello, my name is Chloe Conners and I represent someone who wants to purchase this once glorious diner. My client plans to fully restore Pop's Diner to its original condition," Chloe states as she looks across the table at a man whose life was the diner.

"That would please me. But, my wife of sixty years recently past and this was her life. With the sale of the diner, I feel as though I would sell my memories of her," Ernesto sadly states looking down at the table.

"Ernesto, I am so very sorry for your loss. I remember your wife. Marissa was very charming and kind. She always had a welcoming smile and jovial laugh. As a child, I remember coming here. She would always give me a slice of apple pie," Chloe says as her memories are expressed.

"Yes, she was always kind to children. Marissa became ill many years ago. She struggled with cancer for five years before the fight was lost a couple weeks ago. Now I am at a loss and everywhere is lonely," he struggles with his tears.

"My client was under the impression you were not inclined to sell?" she asks.

"I just do not want this place to become a parking lot," he strongly says.

"Neither does my client," she assures him.

"The mayor wants me to sell it to the city. What is your take on the city buying it?" he asks looking for advice.

"I cannot legally provide you advice for it is a conflict of interest. What I can tell you is that I have a meeting tomorrow with the mayor. I should be able to see the city's plans for buying your place. Will you please give me a week to speak with my client and come up with an offer?" Chloe begs as she places her hand on his.

"Yes, Miss Chloe, I will give you until then!" Ernesto states.

Upon handing him her business card, she gently hugs him.

The taped glass door squeaks as it closes behind her.

Chapter Eleven

Chloe awakens to the sound of her latte machine brewing. She yawns and stretches before walking into the kitchen.

"Good morning, Craig. I did not hear you come in last night," she says upon entering the kitchen.

Her words are met by silence. She looks around to find an empty room but does not panic. Craig has done this before.

Wrapping her hands around the mug, she walks to her balcony. As she leans over the railing, she begins to think about the proposal and the wedding. She dreams of saying I do. As her veil is lifted, Andrea strokes her cheek. "Damn, Andrea get out of my head!" Chloe says as she closes the sliding door behind herself.

She breaks from her routine and hurries to work. She arrives early to an empty office. Placing her briefcase on the desk, she begins to dial her client.

"Good morning, Mr. Griffin. Sorry to call at this hour. If our client is truly serious about this take-over, can you provide an offer for the diner by the end of the day?" she asks.

"Good morning, Miss Conners! I will have it on your desk by one," he calmly answers.

"Thank you, I have a meeting with the mayor at three-thirty today," she provides the reason for the request.

"Will we need another meeting this week?" he inquires.

"Perhaps. Let me look over the plan and have my meeting. I will contact you soon after," she states.

"Very well, I will be in contact with my client this morning," he remarks before ending the call.

She finally opens her briefcase to find the package. Her small hands gently grip the plain wrapped package. As she slowly opens one corner her phone rings.

"Chloe Conner speaking?"

"Hello my dear! How was your night?" Craig asks.

"It was good and how was yours?" she asks.

"It was short. I have meetings all day and a late dinner with a client," he says.

"That's okay, I am playing catch up anyway," she says.

"How about an early dinner tomorrow?" he asks.

"Sure! I'll call you later. Love you," she says.

The quietness slowly ceases as the staff arrives.

Chloe is waiting for Jacob. This is the first time she has sat in the waiting area since her hiring. As the staff shuffle in, she says hello. As Jacob arrives, she follows her mentor to his office. She spends the next hour explaining her client's situation.

"Thank you for the update, Chloe. Just keep me informed about your meeting with the mayor," he says with support.

"Yes, Jacob," Chloe replies as she walks out.

The return path to her office is disrupted by another secretary.

"Excuse me, Chloe. I am going to fill in for Taylor. She called in not feeling well," the middle-aged woman states.

"Okay, Jane, follow me and I will get you situated," Chloe says. "Okay, Jane, my schedule is on her desk. I have one meeting at ten. Then I have a very important meeting at three. Just to make sure, your last name is Smith, correct?" Chloe instructs.

"Yes, it is, and Taylor told me about the three o'clock. I will make sure you are on time. Is there anything else?" she asks in a soft tone.

"Nope, not currently," Chloe says.

Mid-morning arrives and Chloe calls Taylor.

"Hey Tay, how are you feeling?" Chloe asks looking at a file.

"Not good. I think I have a twenty-four-hour bug," Taylor says sniffling

"Do you need me to bring you anything?" Chloe asks.

"Nope, I will be back tomorrow. Is Jane working out for you?" Taylor asks.

"Yes, thank you for selecting her," Chloe says with gratitude.

"You're welcome. See you tomorrow," Taylor says ending the call.

As lunchtime arrives, Chloe emerges from her seclusion.

"So, Jane, have you eaten?" Chloe asks.

"Just about to call you to see if you want something?" Jane answers as the glow from the fluorescent light highlights auburn hair.

"Good, let's go to the deli across the street," Chloe says.

"Really, I have never been asked to lunch by anyone other than the secretaries!" Jane remarks as she removes her purse from the cabinet.

"Really? Taylor and I go about twice a week!" Chloe states with amazement.

As they leave the office, Jane continues the conversation.

"How was your vacation?" her crow's feet show as she looks at the sun.

"It was nice. I enjoyed counseling the youth. I always enjoy the outdoors," Chloe says as she presses the walk button.

"How long have you been part of the camp?" Jane asks as they cross the walk.

"With the exception of college, I have gone there every summer," Chloe says as she opens the door.

"Wow, that is commitment!" Jane says as they take their seats.

"Not really. It is simply doing something you enjoy," Chloe answers as she opens the menu.

The waiter writes their orders down and returns with two glasses of water.

"I am expecting a crucial envelope by one. Please bring it to me immediately," Chloe states after her order arrives.

"Sure thing! Did I see correctly on your calendar that your three thirty-five is with the mayor?" Jane asks.

"Yes, why?" Chloe asks as she bites into her turkey and rye sandwich.

"As I understand, he is a stickler about promptness," she answers.

"Yes, that is why I need you to make sure I am on time. Taylor told me to be there about five minutes early," Chloe says.

"I will make sure you leave twenty minutes early. I do not want you to miss the appointment!" Jane exclaims.

"Good! I am liking you already," Chloe says with a chuckle.

"I now understand why so many secretaries rave about you. You are a great boss," Jane states.

"I don't know about being great. You haven't seen all of my moods," Chloe says humbly.

Jane smiles before sipping on her water.

"So, tell me about your story," Chloe inquires.

"Well, I am a divorcee. My husband shelved me after I had about with the brown bottle. I have two children. I had to start over at the age of fifty. That was tough," Jane says as her brown eyes become watery.

"You know, I think you are doing okay for yourself. If I ever need another secretary, I will demand you," Chloe says.

"Well, thank you for the vote of support," Jane replies.

Chloe glances at her watch.

"My one o'clock will be here soon," Chloe says as she pays the waiter.

"Oh, wow the time flew by," Jane says as she leaves a tip.

They exit the deli to find a limousine stopping in front of the office.

"I think that is your one o'clock," Jane remarks at the black car.

"Perhaps," Chloe answers.

The moment Chloe steps out of the crosswalk and onto the curb, the window lowers on the limousine.

"Hello, Miss Conners. How is your day?" Mr. Griffin asks.

"Hello, Mr. Griffin. Very well!" she replies stepping closer.

"As I promised, here is the updated file along with an offer," handing her the envelope his monotone voice.

Chloe receives the envelope and glances into the car. She's able to see a navy skirt and well-defined tan legs.

"Ok, thank you. I will let you know the outcome of the meeting at three thirty-five," Chloe says as she steps away from the car. The limousine slips back into traffic as she turns away.

As the limousine changes lanes, Mr. Griffin begins to converse.

"Our lawyer is intrigued. She went to the diner yesterday."

"Good. She is being thorough, as I had expected," the voice states.

"Have you moved in yet?" he asks.

"Yes. It was quite relaxing having my own apartment again. I look forward to rattling her confidence once more," the voice states as the car slows.

"I will update you when she calls," he offers as his boss opens the door.

"Henry, please return our friend to the office. I will need you to pick me up here at six," the voice states.

Henry acknowledges with a nod. The boss steps from the car and quickly enters the parking garage.

Chapter Twelve

Chloe calls for a cab as she steps to the curb. She is leaving twenty minutes early as Jane promised. The ride lasts five minutes as the cab stops in front of City Hall. Chloe quickly walks up the marble steps. She enters the mayor's office.

"Hello, I am Chloe Conners. I have a three thirty-five appointment," Chloe says as she holds her briefcase.

"Yes, Miss Conners, I will let him know you are here. Please take a seat," the blonde secretary says.

Chloe smiles and take a seat next to the entrance. As the hands on the clock tick, she reviews the business plan once again. She marvels at the finished design for the diner.

"Excuse me, Miss Conners, he will see you now," the secretary speaks as she leads Chloe inside.

"Hello, Miss Conners. You are a welcome sight so late in the day," the handsome man remarks as he shakes her hand.

"Thank you, Mr. Mayor, for seeing me on such a short notice. I have a demanding client and they want to clarify the notes from the last council meeting," she politely states.

"Well, let's hear the complaint" he asks taking the seat next to her.

"It is not a complaint. My client wants to buy Pop's Diner. The city council denied the sale due to the concern of an outside company displacing local jobs," she explains.

"Yes, I remember that meeting. I too had similar concerns," he reiterates.

"My client has existing ties to the community and is wanting to revitalize the historical diner. They are willing to restore the diner to its original condition," she says handing him the business plan.

"Well, dear, here is the problem. Your client appears to be layered in a 'shell corporation.' And the argument that he or she has existing ties to the community has not be shown. As for revitalizing the diner, I must be shown plans and the owner must approve the plan. Lastly, Miss Conners, the city has an offer to buy the entire block from a local investor," he answers with his hand upon her knee.

"As I understand the situation, first you desire to meet my client to prove the existing ties. Secondly, you need to see the plans. And lastly, you have an existing offer. Did I understand everything?" she asks before removing his hand from her knee.

"Yes," he says as his tone changes.

"I will see about my client's availability to appear. I have the plans right here." As she hands him the envelope, she continues, "And if you have an offer, then that is a matter of public record. Might I see the offer, or shall I have to submit a request?" Chloe sharply states.

He looks at the business plans and the renovation plans. As he stares at them with aggravation, she looks out the window. As her attention is on the pedestrians, he stares at her figure.

"Perhaps, Miss Conner, we should discuss this over dinner?" he adds.

"Sorry Mr. Mayor, that would be inappropriate," she says noticing his glare in the glass.

"Well, if I may keep these, I will submit them to the council and you will not need a written request for the offer. My secretary will mail that by the end of the week. As for your client's appearance, that is not optional. The council will demand meeting this person," he sternly requests.

"Thank you, Mr. Mayor, and I believe this will conclude our business today," Chloe says offering her hand to him.

He returns the offer.

Her narrow hand pushes the door open and she is met by the warm sunshine. She decides to pound the pavement instead of a cab ride. The slight breeze rustles her long, golden-spun hair. Chloe's glowing skin is enriched by the sparkling sun. The pavement is absorbed by her muscular calves. Her stroll takes her past Craig's office building. She crosses the street and dials.

"Hello Honey, how are you today?" Craig's cheerful tone welcomes her.

"Hello, I was just passing by and thought I would call. If you look out across the street, I will wave," she offers.

He walks to the window of the drably-colored conference room.

"How is your day?" she asks leaning against the building.

"Just a second and I will show you," he responds. His hand raises the stripe tie over his sandy-colored hair signaling a noose. "Does that explain it?" he asks as his perfect smile reaches her thin lips.

"Yep. That bad?" she asks.

"I have been in this room since nine researching property laws," his voice dulls as the thought of researching comes to mind.

"Fun. Will I see you tonight?" she begs.

"Probably not until late," he sadly states.

"How about an early dinner?" she suggests.

"Sure. What do you have in mind?" he asks.

"I thought I could pick up take-out and bring it to you. Does pasta sound good?" she says.

"Yes. I will see you at six," he says before waving goodbye.

"I love you," echoes through the line as she waves.

"Love you too," Craig replies.

She continues her path.

Block after block, her destination becomes closer. As she steps inside the doors of the firm, a charcoal Jaguar pulls in front. The occupants begin a conversation.

"What did you learn from Seattle?" the driver asks.

"He is returning this weekend," the raven-haired man in the passenger seat answers.

"This will be the fourth time this month?" the driver asks.

"Still looking into it. What happens if my suspicion for the frequent visits is right?" he asks as his hand accepts the small sealed envelope.

"What are you suspecting?" the driver asks as Chloe enters her office.

"Nothing concrete yet, but if I had to venture a guess? An affair," he says.

"Gather all information. I will determine the next step when everything is known," the driver says as the Jaguar re-enters traffic.

Chloe steps out of her navy heels and removes her pinstriped suit jacket. She leans back in the leather high back chair and places her tired feet on the corner of her desk. Her telephone rings.

"Chloe Conners, how may I help you?" she speaks.

"Hello, my child, how are you?" her mother asks.

"Hi Mom. I have had an exhausting day. How is your day?" she asks.

"Well, it has been hectic. I have been on the phone all day looking for a venue for the reception. I think I found one," she answers.

"You did? Where?" Chloe excitedly asks.

"It is the hall in Government Camp. It is relatively smaller in comparison to those in Portland, but it is very romantic," her mother Ruth remarks.

"Yes, I was just in town before camp started. It is a quaint place," Chloe says as her thoughts revert to the recent past.

"Have you talked to Pastor Richmond?" Ruth asks.

"Nope, I have not had a chance," Chloe answers.

"Will you allow me to do so?" her mother pleads.

"Yes, let me talk to Craig first. I will call you tonight or tomorrow. I love you, Mom. I have to go," Chloe says.

"Love you too, Clo," Ruth says.

Returning the receiver to its cradle, she thinks about the aroma of the cedar bench as she awaits the train. The legs pass by as she is engrossed in her messages. The two words that shook her still waltz in her thoughts.

"Hello, Chloe."

Her eyes work their way up her long legs. Her eyes are locked onto an hour-glass body. Chloe interrupts her stare to continue ascending her eyes. As their eyes finally meet, Chloe shies away from a prolonged look. Her heart pounds with desire as her stoic demeanor remains. "Hey," was all she could utter in her thoughts. As they drove through town, lasciviousness nearly over took her self-control. Her hand wanted to wander to Andrea's tan firm knee as it had eight years earlier. As the stoplight halted their progress, Chloe thought about kissing her, yet the fear of public display and outcry contained her passion. The desires have always been with each woman she has met. Chloe closes the shutter on the window leading to that world and forces her wants to conform to the social world she belongs to. Her dreams recede as her telephone rings.

"Chloe speaking."

"Hello dear, I am sorry to say…" Craig begins speaking.

"Hello, let me guess. You have to go to Seattle again?" Chloe interrupts.

"Yes, it was last minute," he apologetically says.

"How long this time?" she coldly asks.

"Until late Sunday," he says.

"Mom has the reception booked. She wants to know if we have talked to the pastor," Chloe states trying to control her disappointment.

"What did you tell her?" he inquires.

"No. She said she would talk to him if we did not have time," Chloe adds.

Craig remains silent as her words continue.

"I told her I would let her know after we talked tonight. But since that is not going to take place, I will tell her to hold off," Chloe sharply remarks.

"Don't be angry. I cannot help this," he pleads.

"How can I not be angry? We have not spent any time together in the last month," she projects her disappointment.

"You're the one that left for two weeks, not me," he dredges up.

"And you have spent the last six out of the eight weekends in Seattle," she returns the comment.

"Look, I don't want to argue. I am sorry about the late notice. I will call you when I arrive. Love you," he concedes.

"You're right. I am sorry also. I love you. Have a safe flight," she agrees.

For the next five weeks, Chloe devotes minimal free time toward her wedding as October is ushered in.

Chapter Thirteen

The crowd at Hartsfield-Jackson Atlanta International Airport is dense as usual. Andrea just added to the population as she steps from her flight. Her normal subdued temperament is interrupted by a call.

"Andrea Parker speaking," her groggy tone says.

"Miss Parker, I am sorry to say that your mother 's health has taking a turn," the female nurse states.

"Okay, I just landed in Atlanta. It will take me a few hours," Andrea speaks as her thoughts become distant. She steps up to the ticket window and see a familiar face.

"Hello, Miss Andrea. Didn't I just see you yesterday?" the round African American agent states.

"Yes, Latisha, you did. I just got a call my mother's health has taken a turn and I am needed in Portland right away," Andrea says.

"I have a flight leaving in an hour. It is a direct flight to Portland. You'll be there by six. Will this work for you?" she asks.

"Yes, how much time do I have before the flight?" Andrea asks as her thoughts become clouded.

"About an hour. Why don't you grab a bite and relax for a little while?" Latisha asks.

"I think I will," Andrea says as her hand grips the handle of her red carry-on. As she makes her way to a McDonald's, the past flashes in Andrea's thoughts.

Carrying her dinner to the gate, Andrea thinks about the tumultuous relationship with her mother. And she also recalls the healing and repair they were able to make once her parents divorced. She decides to call Erma.

"Hello Andrea, how are you?" Erma kindly asks.

"Not good. My mom is dying, and I am five hours away in Atlanta waiting on a flight. I should be there by six," Andrea rambles.

"Andrea, slow your thoughts and breathe. You are about to panic and there is nothing you can do about this. You cannot control her passing. I will sit with her until you arrive," Erma consoles her.

"Thank you," Andrea states as her flight is called.

"You're welcome. I will see you at around six," Erma says as she grabs her car keys.

As her tired legs board the plane, she remembers to call her staff.

"Margery, my mom, is not well and I am returning to Portland. I am not sure of the duration this time," Andrea says as she takes her seat.

"Andrea, we have this. Just take care of yourself. I will call if anything needs your attention," her secretary states.

"Thank you," Andrea says. With her phone now on flight status, she rests her head against the window. As the ground lowers beneath the ascending plane, she thinks about her life.

The moment her father found a younger woman was the opportunity she had waited for. As her mother was devastated by his abandonment, Andrea stepped in and paid for her attorney. Her father tried to trick Allison into signing the agreement. Andrea re-emerged from seclusion to prevent his bullying. He was not pleased to see her. He wanted to maintain his public appearance and status. For him to do so, Andrea blackmailed him into signing three quarters of their assets to her mother.

Their divorce was recorded as amicable. His infidelity went undocumented. The patches of green and brown pass below as she stares out the window. Her thoughts carry her exhausted body into a dream. Her mahogany brown hair rests against the window. Andrea's dreams come rushing back as the white cotton clouds float by. Her mind returns to Chloe and how captivated she has been with her for years. Chloe's ash blonde hair rests on the paint-chipped oak picnic table as Andrea lies next to her. With hands touching, Andrea allows Chloe into her world. Her longing desires and faith in destiny has her believing Chloe is her future. Andrea fell in love with Chloe at first sight. Each day brought new reassurances that Chloe was the one. The night on the dock when Chloe told her there was no *next* ended her belief in destiny. After that day, her desires only filled with the physical. Andrea has had several encounters, yet only one other had penetrated the level Chloe did.

The flight lands on schedule. As the passengers file out, Andrea rushes past the lollygaggers and out to a car waiting for her. Margery had called ahead for car service. The driver zips through traffic. He unloads her luggage. She walks into the nursing home where she is met by a pungent odor. The health center uses a strong sanitizer to clean with. She hurries into the private room. Erma greets Andrea with a hug.

"She is still hanging on! Go be at her side. I am going to step out for a bit. Do you need anything?" Erma asks.

"No, thank you. Will you be back?" Andrea asks staring at the woman she spent most of her life hating.

"If you want me to," Erma says resting her wrinkled hand on Andrea's shoulder.

"Yes," Andrea affirms.

"Then I will give you some time," Erma says as Andrea stares at Allison gasping for a breath.

Andrea carefully approaches her mother. Taking her hand, Andrea realizes she is soon to be alone. Her mother was the remaining family she had. After the car accident, Andrea was left with memories. Her chestnut eyes tear as the loneliness engulfs the quiet room. Finally given into her emotions, Andrea takes a seat against the wall.

An hour languishes by as the brunette sits quietly rummaging through the bad feelings and the reconciliation they had achieved. Allison's breath becomes gargled. The final few breaths are coming.

Suddenly, Allison's chest rises and falls with her last breath leaving her. Andrea sits hearing the final gasp over and over as she cries. From the hall, Andrea is heard shouting, "No, don't go!"

Allison's exit has left Andrea doubled in the chair as her hands cradle her guilt-stricken thoughts. The tears seep through her fingers falling onto her lap. Her crying increases when a set of hands rest on her thighs as she falls apart. The person allows her to slide into her awaiting arms. Andrea slowly gathers herself to find the ash blonde hair meshed with hers. As she rises, Andrea finds Chloe holding her. Their eyes meet, and a long stare fills the air.

"Excuse me, Miss Parker, it is time," the nurse says.

Realizing Andrea is distraught, Chloe places her warm hands on Andrea's red cheeks and speaks.

"Andrea, let her go," Chloe says as she helps her from the room.

Erma watches on as Chloe consoles her.

"I'm okay, just didn't fathom her passing would affect me like that," Andrea says as Chloe stands next to her.

"She is your mother. Why would it not affect you?" Chloe says taking her hand.

"Andrea, I am so sorry. Is there anything I can do?" Erma injects.

"No, everything is paid for. I took care of that a couple years ago when she fell ill the first time," Andrea remarks as her stoic composure returns.

"Do you want go somewhere?" Chloe asks.

"Yeah, back to eight years ago. I would undo almost everything," Andrea says as the shock wears off.

Sensing a time for silence, Chloe and Erma allow the comment to drift away.

"I need a drink," Andrea says to Erma.

As they walk away, Chloe remains behind.

"Are you coming?" Andrea says with a slight grin.

"Sure," Chloe says as she follows.

As her carry-on is placed in the back of the Pathfinder, Andrea opens the door for Erma. Erma struggles to lift her short, pudgy frame onto the passenger seat. Andrea smiles as a grunt leaves Erma's lips. As Chloe steps into the driver's side she glances at Andrea. Andrea is sitting behind Erma.

"This is a really big vehicle," Erma remarks.

"It is said that larger vehicles are a sign of over-compensating," Andrea says as she looks out the window.

"Yeah, don't think that applies here," Chloe says with a glance in the rearview mirror at the person she once had feelings for.

"Never know," Andrea says as she stares at the last place her mother was alive.

"I am pretty sure I do not have any inadequacies," Chloe states.

"Except your ego," Erma says.

"Point taken," Chloe says as she passes the courthouse.

Andrea notices Chloe's engagement ring as she grips the leather steering wheel.

"How's the planning going?" she inquires leaning forward between the seats.

"Okay. Mom has done most of it," Chloe answers as she looks at Andrea.

"Why is that? I thought you would be neck high in the details," Erma remarks.

"I have been busy with a client and the battle with the city council," Chloe says as the lines around her cheek show.

"That must be a hassle. How's the fight going?" Andrea asks.

"Too soon to tell," she replies as the Pathfinder pulls onto a lot.

Andrea offers Erma an arm as she steps out.

"Thank you for calling her," Andrea says taking in the cool air.

"I thought *you* called her," Erma states.

With an inquisitive look, they walk toward the entrance. Chloe is slightly shorter than Andrea. Andrea notices her figure as she walks a few strides ahead. Feeling the stare, Chloe turns to smile at them.

"Hey, can I have a few minutes?" Andrea says before entering.

"Yeah," Erma says turning to watch Andrea walk toward the park.

"I'll be right back. Go on inside and order me a Rum and Coke. We will be there shortly," Chloe says.

Her steps follow Andrea. Andrea reaches a bench where her shocked spirit takes a seat. Chloe hesitates to join her until Andrea begins to cry. Stepping over the seat, Chloe sits close to her sobbing love.

"Let it out, Andrea," Chloe says wrapping her arm around her.

"I am now all alone," she hauntingly realizes.

"No, you're not," Chloe says pulling Andrea against her shoulder.

"I have no family, barely a few real friends, and no one to come home to now," Andrea says regaining her control.

The slight wind blows a distant ship whistle past.

"After the funeral is over, I probably will not return to Portland," Andrea says acknowledging defeat in any hope her return may have given her.

"What about Erma? She is our family!" Chloe exclaims removing her arm as a couple passes.

"What about you? Is there any future here? Please, anything at all?" Andrea asks noticing Chloe's response to the passing couple.

"Andrea, I can't. But I also cannot deny the obvious attraction between us. Your mother has just passed, so just give your emotions some time to settle. Let's go. It is getting cool," Chloe says stepping over the seat.

Heads turn as Chloe and Andrea enter. Chloe's fairing complexion and Andrea's well-tanned narrow cheeks cause a slight glance from the other customers. As they join Erma, Andrea looks around.

"Didn't this use to be a dive called the Pelican?"

"Yes, it was purchased a year ago and is now a hot spot," Chloe says. The cold wooden chairs shock Andrea as her bare legs rest on it.

"Damn wooden chairs. Forgot how cold they are!" Andrea says as she places a napkin under her legs. After Andrea's drink order is taken, Chloe starts the conversation.

"Andrea, I did not ask you what you do in Atlanta."

"I am a criminal attorney," she says.

"How is the practice?" Erma asks.

Chloe is impressed with Andrea and wants so desperately to touch her hand.

"Things are good. I just returned to Atlanta when I got the call," Andrea adds when a growl erupts.

Chloe hands her a menu.

"Thanks," Andrea says as she reviews it.

"Where were you returning from?" Chloe asks.

"Miami," Andrea says as she decides.

"Were you successful?" Erma asks.

"Yes. My client was acquitted," Andrea answers. The waiter returns. "I want to order the fish tacos and a side of chips," she says.

"Anything for you ladies?" the young man asks.

Erma orders the wings and fries and Chloe orders nachos.

"What is Miami like?" Chloe asks.

"A hot bed of culture where the women are sexy. My client was well-tanned and Latino. Her name is Miami. Her case was in the Keys. Sexy cannot even begin to describe her," Andrea says hoping to spark a response from Chloe.

"Was that your payment?" Chloe asks as she takes the bait.

"Perhaps," Andrea remarks with a shitty grin as she proceeds to look at Chloe.

"Well, that is enough of that!" Erma says.

Their dinner is served.

The conversation slows when Andrea orders her third shot.

"I have no idea how to handle the funeral," Andrea says as her mood darkens with the assist of the whiskey. They watch as her chestnut eyes darken. As her phone rings, Andrea notices the number. "Excuse me, I have to take this." Her hand brushes Chloe's as she steps away.

"Erma, is she alright?" Chloe asks as she watches her demeanor from the window.

"Hard to tell. Not sure you want to attend the funeral. It may get messy, especially if her father appears," Erma says with concern.

"Why would he appear?" Chloe asks.

"He is a narcissist," she says.

"Can Andrea handle this right now?" Chloe asks as she watches Andrea's temper boil.

"She will have to," Erma answers as the waiter returns.

"Will there be another round?"

"No thank you," Erma states noticing Andrea returning.

Taking her seat, Andrea fights the tears once more. Chloe sees the anger and sadness clashing in her eyes. She reaches for her cold hand.

"Excuse me, I need to freshen up," Andrea says removing her hand from the table.

Chloe watches as she disappears into the restroom.

"Excuse me," Chloe says as she follows her.

"Go get her," Erma remarks.

As the water splashes from her narrow cheeks, Andrea covers her face with her hands. Chloe is standing behind her. Andrea is stunned at the sight of Chloe. Chloe walks up to her and wraps her arms around Andrea. Resting her head against Andrea's, Chloe tightens her grip. With her arms lowered, Andrea closes her red eyes and allows the moment to happen. After several minutes, she loosens Chloe's hands and walks out.

Returning to the table, Andrea makes a statement.

"Erma, I am really exhausted. Please tell Chloe thank you for me."

"Do you have a place to stay?" Erma asks as she takes her hand.

"Yes, I have things to take care of tomorrow, so I am going to turn in. I will call when the final arrangements are made," Andrea says. She kisses Erma on the cheek and hurries out. Chloe returns to find Andrea gone.

"Did she leave?"

"Yes, she was tired and needed some rest. She summoned a cab," Erma answers.

"Did she say where she was staying?" Chloe subtly asks.

"Nope, only she has a place," Erma says as she stands.

"Waiter, can we get the check?" Chloe asks as she reaches in her purse.

"Your friend already paid," he said before walking away.

"Okay, thank you. Are you ready to go?" Erma asks.

"Yes, I have a full day ahead tomorrow," Chloe answers with a yawn.

Climbing into her Pathfinder, Erma grunts once more before commenting.

"What happened in the restroom?" she asks.

"Nothing," Chloe says.

"I have never seen Andrea as vulnerable as she was tonight," Erma states.

"Well, considering she just lost her mother, I would say she has a right to be distraught," Chloe's quick defensive comment made Erma smile. "Why are you smiling?" Chloe demands politely.

"Your instantaneous response. I think you still have feelings for her," Erma declares.

"I do, but as a friend only," Chloe remarks holding steadfast to the facade she has fought to maintain.

"Sure," Erma says.

Chloe tightens her grip on the steering wheel attempting to hide her desires. As they arrive at the nursing home, Chloe assists Erma.

A question flows to Chloe's rambling thoughts.

"You said at camp that you have been in contact with Andrea through the years. Did you she ever ask about me?"

"Always! You know she always thought about you. Her tone changed when your name came up," Erma answers watching Chloe's facial reaction.

"Are you capable of driving home?" Chloe asks.

"Yes, my dear, I will be fine. Are you going to attend the funeral?" Erma asks as she digs for her keys.

"Depends," Chloe says.

"Depends on what? She is your friend as you just declared," Erma sternly states.

"My schedule and when Craig returns from Seattle," Chloe says.

"Oh, I forgot, you have an image to keep! I will let you know the times and you can make your decision. Goodnight, my other child," Erma says.

Chloe hugs her. She watches as the compact car drives away. Her glance at the nursing home becomes a stare. The rain streaks down her white blouse soaking her. With exposure of her white lace bra, Chloe's wanting blue eyes lock on the sight of Andrea standing inside. She is conversing with a nurse while holding a box. The cold rain chills her small breast as her stare goes uninterrupted. Andrea steps out to find Chloe's ash blonde hair darkened by the downpour. She pauses to allow her eyes to absorb the sight of her bra piercing the white blouse. Andrea strolls to a cab unaffected by the cold rain. She smiles at Chloe and turns to open the car door. She places the box on the floorboard. Chloe runs to meet Andrea on the passenger side. Her attempt to open the door becomes futile as Chloe places her hand on Andrea's. Chloe pulls Andrea against her as the rain continues. Andrea's dark hair rests on her shoulders. Andrea hastily turns to face Chloe. She shoves Chloe against the SUV. With a show of force, Chloe returns the shove. Andrea grips Chloe's fit waist and walks her against the SUV. Their eyes meet as the rain pounds their desires. Chloe places her thin hands on Andrea's defined cheeks. She steps in allowing her opulent lips to rest against Andrea's thin red lips. Chloe opens her lips to allow her tongue to slide across. Andrea removes Chloe's cold hands and steps away.

"Goodnight," Andrea softly says as she opens the car door.

Chloe falls against the Pathfinder slamming her palm against the passenger door. "God damn it, Andrea. Get out of my fucking desires!" Chloe walks to the driver's side and leaves soon after.

Chapter Fourteen

The next couple of days finds Chloe preparing for the city council meeting. She has spent several hours working with her mentor and boss Jacob.

"Have you been in contact with Mr. Griffin?" he asks as the meeting ends.

"Yes, he has reassured me that his client will appear at the meeting Friday evening," she answers.

"Good, because the last thing you will want to do is waste this opportunity," he sternly advises.

"I agree! Will you be there?" she asks.

"No, you can handle this," he says with support.

"Yeah, I can," she remarks before leaving.

As she returns to her office. Taylor hands Chloe her messages while on the phone. The oak door closes behind her. She places the messages on her desk and pours a cup of coffee. The swirls circle the cup as she pours the creamer in. The steam rises and tantalizes her thoughts with confusion. She loves Craig, but desires Andrea. She has no one to discuss her conflict with. Chloe remembers how her parents reacted to the introduction of Andrea on family day at the camp. Her mother saw a troubled young lady. Her father saw a young lady without any purpose. They shunned the friendship. When Chloe looked at Andrea, she saw strength and comfort. At the time, she was heavily influenced by goals and achievement. After that Saturday, Chloe started distancing herself from Andrea. Chloe was taking comments from her friends and parents. She was not strong enough to stand up to the peer pressure and follow her heart. She walked away from a person who could have been her future. Now her perfect life and fiancé fit the mold her family and friends accept. The leather high back chair welcomes her as she reaches for the messages.

Her hands pause when the name Erma arrives. The message simply reads, "Call me asap!"

Chloe quickly dials.

"Hello Erma, how are you?"

"Wow, you actually called back the same day!" Erma says referring to her history of returning calls.

"Yep, thought I had better work on that," Chloe says light-heartedly.

"Andrea called. She had to return to Atlanta Tuesday morning. The services are Thursday from four to seven. The funeral is Friday at three at Barclays. Are you going?" Erma asks in an all but begging tone.

"Yes," Chloe answers as she looks at the camp photo.

"Good, I will see you there," Erma says as her voice lightens.

As the call concludes, Taylor knocks.

"Come in," Chloe states.

"Is everything okay with Erma?" she asks.

"Yes. What does my schedule look like Thursday evening?" Chloe asks.

"You have meetings until four and dinner with Craig at six. Why?" Taylor asks as she leans against the desk.

"Can you cancel with Craig? I have a visitation. It starts at four. I will take the meeting and go to the visitation afterwards," Chloe states.

"I will cancel with Craig, but you should really do that," Taylor advises.

"You're right. I will take care of it," Chloe realizes.

"Are you ready for the council meeting?" Taylor asks.

"I think so," she answers.

"Oh, Mr. Griffin is stopping by Thursday around one. That was the only time you had available," Taylor says as she watches Chloe getting lost in thought. "Did you hear me?" Taylor inquires.

"No, sorry," Chloe says.

"What is going on? You have been distracted since yesterday," Taylor says.

"The mother of a friend from camp passed away two nights ago. You know seeing a person actually heartbroken can rattle anyone," Chloe says as she feels Andrea in her arms.

"I am sorry to hear that. Is your friend okay?" Taylor adds.

Noticing Chloe's emotions, Taylor just looks away.

"Not sure. Perhaps time will help. Did you say Mr. Griffin is stopping by Thursday?" Chloe asks as her thoughts clear.

"Yes," Taylor answers tucking her strawberry blonde hair behind her ear.

"Okay," Chloe say.

"Don't forget about calling Craig," Taylor reminds her.

The door closes behind Taylor as the silence returns. Chloe allows her schedule to pre-occupy her thoughts. She spends the evening rehearsing the council meeting.

Thursday arrives to find Chloe with mixed emotions about seeing Andrea in a crowd setting. Chloe is afraid the world will know her secret if she looks at Andrea. Unsure of her ability to control the desire to touch Andrea, Chloe has second thoughts about attending the services. As the sudden thought comes to mind, she suddenly remembers she forgot to cancel with Craig.

"Oh shit!" she says as her finger hastily dials his number.

"Well, hello. Did you not get enough last night that you have to call so soon?" he seductively asks.

"What?" Chloe says.

"Sorry, Chloe I was joking," Craig says as he realizes his mistake.

"I forgot to cancel our dinner tonight. I have a visitation to attend," she somberly says.

"It is no problem. Who is the visitation for?" he suddenly changes his tone.

"A mother of a friend from camp passed. The visitation is tonight, and the funeral is tomorrow," Chloe answers with thoughts of Andrea.

"Do I know this friend?" he asks with suspicion.

"I do not believe so," she answers.

"Do you want me to go with you?" he offers.

"Thank you, but that is not necessary. I will be fine," she quickly dismisses his offer.

"Okay, I can stop by later," he offers.

"I'll let you know." Chloe says before ending the call.

Her morning passes slowly as she looks across the conference room table at her most loathed client.

"Okay, Mr. Norman, here is the status of your offer," she says hoping he will remain seated.

"Your take-over offer is countered. They want four hundred thousand," she states.

"I am prepared to counter with three hundred thousand and not a penny more," he firmly states as his arms lift him from the chair.

She whispers to herself, Oh God here he comes! She immediately excuses herself. He stops his forward approach as she leaves the room.

"OMG, I nearly escaped that one!" Chloe says as leans against the wall around the corner from the conference room.

"What are you doing?" Jacob inquires at the sight of her hiding.

"It is the Norman effect and he was approaching me," she says with disgust. Jacob giggles at her reaction. "He offered a counter and I used that as my excuse to leave the room," she says looking at her watch.

"Okay, let's go. I can help you," Jacob says grinning.

Entering the room, he is leaning against the window ledge.

"Oh hello, Jacob. I did not expect to see you," he adds after changing his demeanor.

"Hello, Mr. Norman. I thought I would drop by to say hello," Jacob says.

"I stepped out to send the counter offer. I will be in contact after they have reviewed it. So, I will leave the two of you to converse. Mr. Norman it is good to see you again. Jacob, thank you for reviewing the offer," Chloe says as she dashes out. She is met half-way to her office by Taylor.

"So, do you need a shower?" Taylor comments as she laughs at his actions.

"Nope, avoided that one," Chloe remarks as they pass the waiting room.

In one movement she stops and steps back to see Mr. Griffin waiting.

"Hello, Mr. Griffin, come on back," Chloe says cheerfully. His tall lanky frame follows as she opens the door for him. "Please have a seat. I noticed you had schedule an unusual time. Is there anything wrong?" she asks taking the seat next to him.

"No, my client is pleased with your performance and is looking forward to meeting you. We do not expect any decision tonight. My client would like to have an early dinner with you to get to know you and have a face to place with the name. I have been very supportive of your abilities. In doing so, my client has agreed to meet you. This does not happen often in contract issues," his monotone voice states.

"I look forward to finally meeting the client," she happily adds.

"Very well, Miss Conners, until tomorrow," the pale, older gentleman confirms.

She takes his outstretched hand and shakes it. He quietly leaves the office.

As her last appointment arrives, so does her nerves. She is anxious about seeing Andrea again, yet wishing it was under different circumstances. She is glad the last appointment is with her favorite client.

"Mr. and Mrs. Brewer, it is so good to see you again," she says. They were her first clients. She resolved a contract dispute with his business partner.

"Miss Chloe, congratulations are in store. I was happy to read the announcement. You're such a beautiful person. I hope the future blesses the road ahead for you," Betty Brewer comments.

"Well, thank you very much. Would you like an invitation to the wedding?" Chloe cheerfully asks.

"Why yes, my dear! We would very much like to be there!" Betty says.

"Sure, now what brings you here today?" Chloe asks as she sits on the end of her desk.

"We're thinking about semi-retiring and want to turn over the day-to-day operations to Ritchie. However, we will still oversee the financial responsibilities for at least a year," Herbert states.

"Ritchie will be a great manager. I think a year should be sufficient to determine his abilities. I also believe it is a great decision to oversee the finances. Sometimes baby steps are the best. I will draw up a preplan and have you review it. This will take a couple weeks," Chloe says as she swings her legs like a child.

"That will work wonderfully for us," Herbert says gladly.

"Where is the honeymoon going to be?" Betty asks.

"I think we may wait until spring, but I am not sure," Chloe answers.

"Maybe somewhere exotic?" Betty hints.

Chloe chuckles at her sweet smile.

"Okay Chloe, we must be going. Do not forget about the invitation," Herbert states offering Betty his hand.

"I won't. I will be in contact about the contract," Chloe says as she walks them out.

They hug her as Taylor looks on.

As Chloe glances at Taylor, Taylor points to the clock. Chloe hurries to her private restroom to fresh up. A half-hour later, Chloe emerges wearing a knee length black skirt with a light gray silk shirt and black suit jacket. She slips on her black heels with a gray tip on the toe.

"How do I look?" Chloe asks looking at Taylor.

"You look nice," she answers as Chloe twirls slowly.

"All right, Taylor, I am leaving. If you need anything, just call," Chloe says.

"Will do, Clo. Take care," Taylor says as Chloe removes her raincoat from the hall tree.

Summoning a cab, she offers a large tip if he arrives before five-thirty. Her offer sparks a sense of urgency as the accelerator lowers. As the rain drops fall, the cab comes to a stop at the funeral home. She passes the large elm trees flanking the walkway. The breeze blows the drops across her as she hurries up the concrete steps. Her heart is racing with anticipation as well as sadness. She removes her raincoat and hands it to the gentleman at the door. The heavy scent of roses over-shadows her anticipation. Her nerves settle as a crowded room awaits her. She knows some of the sympathizers. Her bright blues eyes search the room for Andrea. As the monitor displays memories of Andrea with her mother and sister, Chloe is taken back by the striking beauty of Andrea when she was young. Deep in thought, Chloe is unaware of Erma's arrival.

"I am glad you made it," Erma says as she touches Chloe's arms.

"How is Andrea?" Chloe asks as her attention is diverted to Erma.

"After her father arrived, Andrea has been MIA. The two of them loudly argued before he was escorted out," Erma explains.

"Where is she?" Chloe inquires.

"I think she stepped out," Erma says.

"I'll be right back," Chloe says stepping away.

Chloe searches for the person she held two days ago.

Stepping outside, Chloe sees the figure of the person she knew eight years earlier. With apprehension, Chloe slowly approaches the veranda. Joining her at the rail, Chloe speaks.

"Are you okay?"

"No, but do I have a choice?" Andrea says with a hint of anger and edge.

"Erma told me about your father's presence. I am sorry," with her hand touching Andrea's, Chloe steps closer.

Andrea closes her brown eyes allowing Chloe's touch to reach her. Raising her head, Andrea stares at Chloe with a tear falling. A sensation to speak begins to air from Andrea's lips as they separate. Chloe simply wipes the tear away and caresses Andrea's cheek. Slipping her hand from under Chloe's, Andrea places her hand on Chloe's waist. The cool crisp air is warmed by the desire in their stare. The moment is interrupted by the ding on Chloe's phone.

"Sorry," Chloe says stepping away from a tender moment. Chloe stops momentarily at the doorway and stares once more.

Chloe finds Erma.

"Where did you go?" Erma asks with suspicion.

"I took my phone to the car," Chloe says not wanting to share that moment. "Would you join me as I view her mother?" Chloe asks.

"Yes," Erma says as she takes Chloe by the arm. Making their way around the room and up to the bronze casket, Chloe manages hellos to those she knows. As Allison's body rests peacefully, Chloe notices the resemblance of Andrea in her mother's features.

"Andrea looks quite a bit like her mom," Chloe remarks.

"Yes, they have the same cheek bones and hair color. Andrea was slightly taller than her," Erma adds.

They step away to allow others to view her. Andrea enters the room from the patio doors. Chloe immediately notices her puffy eyes and paler complexion. The darkness on the veranda made her appearance vague. Fighting the desire to run to her, Chloe maintains her distance.

As the room continues to fill, Chloe notices a young lady at Andrea's side. The shorter blonde-haired woman wraps her arm around Andrea's waist as they circle the room. Chloe's heart is crushed as her desire is dampened. Erma tries to increase her pace while Chloe slows hers. As the distance shortens, Andrea locks eyes with Chloe. Chloe looks away and Andrea continues the stare.

"Hello Erma and Chloe, I am so glad you made it," Andrea says as she embraces Erma.

Chloe's fear prevents her from stepping closer. Andrea reaches for Chloe as she remains distant. Erma all but forces her advancement toward Andrea. Andrea wraps her toned arms around Chloe and whispers, "Thank you for coming. You look beautiful. Thank you for a few minutes ago."

"I am sorry for your loss. Is there anything I can do for you?" Chloe asks as she breaks the chill within her disappointment.

"Maybe later," Andrea says as her cheek brushes Chloe's.

Andrea returns to her previous position next to the woman.

"Let me introduce you to Ridley. She is very special to me," Andrea says.

Ridley offers her hand to Erma and then Chloe.

"Nice to meet you. Andrea has mentioned the both of you often. She is very fond of you," Ridley comments.

"She is like a daughter to me!" Erma states with a fondness in her eyes.

"We became friends eight years ago in camp," Chloe remarks as she shoots Andrea a glance.

"She was an antagonist to me. But somehow, a friendship came from the competition," Chloe continues.

"She mentioned how competitive you are," Ridley remarks in a clear Bronx tone.

"How did you two come to meet?" Chloe asks wanting to pry.

"We met outside a club. We've been close since," Ridley says as her young face expresses gratitude.

"I am happy you are not alone during this time," Erma says.

Chloe smiles as the sympathizers grow.

"Well, I can see you have well-wishers awaiting you. It is nice to meet you Ridley. Andrea, take care and if there is anything I can do, feel free to ask," Chloe says as she steps away.

Andrea tries to look away as Chloe steps out.

She arrives home to find Craig lounging on the sofa with a glass of Scotch.

"Hello Honey, how was the visitation?" he asks rising to greet her.

"It was really crowded. I was able to see a dear friend from camp. It was her mother that passed," Chloe adds before they embrace.

Her desires for Andrea pour from her blues eyes as she struggles with her feelings.

"I am sorry for your friend's loss. I could not imagine losing a parent," he says supporting her.

"Being there tonight has made me realize how much I have missed. Why is it that death has a way of humbling even the most hardened person?" Chloe rhetorically asks.

He remains silent as she pulls away. Chloe walks to the kitchen where a bottle of Merlot is waiting. An hour passes, as the wine saturates her sobriety, she becomes angry at the struggle within. He grabs her arm and yanks her to the bedroom. As the anger and desires meet, he forces himself on her.

Chapter Fifteen

Another day of a rain-soaked pavement splashes beneath Chloe's flats as she hurries into her office building. She shakes the water from her raincoat as thunder clasps. November has arrived by two days and the weather is chilling her bones. She passes Taylor as her arms shiver.

"Good morning, Chloe," Taylor says as she passes.

"Give me ten and bring your note pad," Chloe says as she rushes by. She sits on the leather sofa allowing her feet to dry. Taylor knocks before entering.

"Good morning, Taylor. Has your investigation into Andrea Parker panned out?" Chloe says as she dries her feet with a hand towel.

"I was finally able to discover that her successful law practice has several high- profile clients. She has also mentored several homeless children. One of her programs is for teenagers only. These lost or discarded souls have been provided food and shelter. There is very little about her private life. What is she to you?" Taylor asks as she leans against the desk.

"Her name came up," Chloe answers.

"What time are you leaving for the funeral?" Taylor asks.

"About two. I should be able to return by four. My council meeting is at six, so I should have enough time to fresh up," Chloe says.

"Okay, I will make sure after lunch your schedule remains clear," Taylor speaks before heading out. "Oh, by the way, did you ever open that gift?" Taylor asks.

"Oh crap, thanks for reminding me!" Chloe says as Taylor closes the door.

Chloe makes her way around the desk and retrieves the gift from her safe. The unassuming plain wrapped box is placed on her glass top. Chloe looks at it as she gets lost in thought. Her dreams return her to the second time Andrea challenged her. It was the opening day and the schedule was being read.

"Ok guides, there are some changes to the schedule. Chloe, your team will share the canoeing with Andrea's team!" Erma states as Chloe's look of superiority slips from her face.

"How is that going to work?" Chloe remarks.

"It is called teamwork!" Andrea sharply replies.

"My team should not have to share with any other," Chloe demands.

"Why, have you forgotten how? You know, we have children here that can give you a refresher," Andrea antagonizes.

"That will be enough! You will share and that is the last of it!" Erma scolds them.

The teams make their way to the canoes. Chloe shoves off. She drops the paddle in the early morning cold lake and splatters Andrea. As Chloe paddles quickly around the dock, Andrea chases after. The calm water carries the canoe from the shallows. Andrea meets it at the edge of the dock. Unbeknownst to Chloe, Andrea is waiting for the front of the canoe to pass. As Chloe paddles by, Andrea tips the canoe and drops Chloe in the cold water. When Chloe rises, her eyeliner is streaking down her cheeks.

"Now do you want to keep playing?" Andrea says as the water splashes her white t-shirt.

Andrea walks away as Chloe stands in waist-high water embarrassed. The cold water recedes into her memories and Chloe finds herself smiling. She finally met her match.

The box sits waiting for her hands to open it. Chloe returns her attention to the box. The featherlight box has her interest peaked as she rattles it. Slowly her nervous hands unwrap the gift. The wrapper falls from the corner and excitement bubbles within her childish nature. Opening the lid, Chloe pulls the tissue paper back. Her excitement settles as the red flag rests in the box. The small envelope rests beneath it. As she tosses the flag on her desk, she knows the signature awaiting her. She carefully opens the plain envelope to find a message:

My dearest Chloe,

I hope you relished the team competition victory.

Congratulations,
A

"Son-of-a!" Chloe says out loud as she caresses the note. She realizes her victory over Andrea is tainted.

She reminisces on and off as the two o'clock hour approaches. Her phone rings.

"Yeah Taylor?" Chloe says.

"It is going on two. You need to be heading out," Taylor reminds her.

Chloe emerges from the office and stops at Taylor's desk.

"How do I look?" Chloe asks as anticipation of seeing Andrea bubbles.

"You look fine! Why are you smiling headed to a funeral?" Taylor asks with a puzzled look.

"I was thinking about the council meeting and I feel really prepared," she lies.

"Okay, be safe and I am really sorry for your friend's loss," Taylor says.

Chloe realizes how warped the smile must have seemed, so she dims her expression. "Thank you!" Chloe says as she slips her raincoat on.

As the rain dwindles to a mist, she walks to her Pathfinder. She notices the red carry-on laying in the back. With the mist covering the windshield, the wipers squeak as they clear away the water. Chloe finds her thoughts drifting in and out as she recalls holding Andrea. With her wedding date closing in, she tries to deny thinking about her perfect life with Craig. Her friends and family are preparing for a beautiful bride and her prince charming. Yet, her desires have other intentions.

The gate appears with a pond on each side. The Pathfinder is halted by a line of cars delivering their passengers.

Finally reaching the lot, the Pathfinder backs into a parking space. She reaches for an umbrella on the floorboard. The black heels approach the white stucco building and all eyes are on her. The men standing outside smoking are gifted with a pair of chiseled legs. Her black heels and skirt are complemented by a white silk blouse and silver scarf.

The strikingly older gentleman opens the door for her. She smiles as a sign of thank you. As the door closes behind her, she approaches the guest registry. Her flared signature decorates the lined paper. The pen rests on the registry as she steps away. Andrea steps from behind the stairway with Ridley in toe. Chloe's hopes dash as she was hoping to speak to Andrea alone. Their paths collide as a glare ensues.

"Hello Chloe, I am glad you could make it," Ridley states opening her arms to the woman she only met a day earlier.

"Hello Ridley, I am glad I could make it as well," Chloe says as their eyes remain locked.

"Excuse me, Miss Parker, may I speak with you in private?" the usher asks.

"Yes," she replies as he escorts her into the other den.

As the crowd corrals Chloe closer to Ridley, they step aside.

"Ridley, how is she really doing?" Chloe asks looking into her softer brown eyes compared to Andrea's darker eyes. As Ridley's lips separate, the question is answered from behind Chloe.

"Why don't you ask yourself?" Andrea coldly interrupts.

Chloe turns around.

"Sorry, I didn't realize you were behind me," Chloe innocently answers.

"Well, I am right here. So, just ask!" Andrea sharply states.

Chloe is taken back by her tone. Andrea stares at Chloe waiting for the question.

"I am sorry if I was out of line," Chloe says as she steps away lowering her blonde head.

Chloe searches for Erma leaving Andrea standing in the hall.

"Andrea, what the hell?" Ridley says.

"I just want her to talk to me and not around me," Andrea remarks.

"You need to apologize. She was simply showing concern. Isn't that what you wanted?" Ridley scolds her before leaving her in the hall.

Andrea allows Ridley's words to settle before searching for Chloe.

The music chimes as the video of Allison replays. Chloe is chatting with Erma attempting to hide her hurt. As Andrea approaches, Erma glances in her direction. Chloe notices the glance and walks away. Andrea joins Erma.

"Now what happened? Did she say something wrong?" Erma says assuming Chloe is the culprit.

"No, I was hateful to her," Andrea says.

"I am sure you are just in mourning," Erma states.

"I am, but I was a bitch to her. She did not deserve it," Andrea says as she disciplines her actions.

"Well, go tell her how you feel," Erma urges.

Andrea slowly makes her way through the crowd and searches for Chloe. Chloe steps out onto the veranda off the side of the room. As the mist settles into the evergreens, Chloe stares out toward the city. With tears welling, she wills them not to fall. The words Andrea spoke are seeping into her heart. A feeling a stupidity comes over her as she hangs onto the railing.

"I'm sorry," Andrea states as she watches Chloe lower her head.

"Go away! I am just catching my breath and then I'll be gone!" Chloe says as she looks up.

Andrea remains speechless but steps closer. Chloe turns to leave. Andrea walks Chloe against the cold stucco and stares at her.

"I came here out of care. But it is obvious you do not need me or my concern so, I must go. I am tired of this game. Have a good life. I have a marriage to prepare for," Chloe speaks as her tears build. She steps around Andrea and walks away.

"Chloe, please don't go! I love you!" Andrea's words break in her tone as Chloe stops at the corner.

Chloe's pause ceases as her feet step on.

Chloe's brisk pace carries her past Erma and Ridley as they see her tears. They are stunned to see Andrea sprinting after her. Stopped by well-wishers, Andrea's pace is slowed. She removes the carry-on. Rolling it to the white limousine, the driver greets her.

"Is this the limousine for Andrea Parker?" she asks as the mist thickens.

"Yes," the driver answers.

Chloe lowers the handle and leaves it in front of him. Andrea hurries to the entrance to find Chloe lowering the handle. Andrea looks on as Chloe walks away. Realizing the hurt she has caused, Andrea remains standing under the covered entrance.

The Pathfinder comes to a stop at the waterfront park. The steering wheel becomes her slapping post as her emotions explode. Her solo conversation begins.

"Why Chloe would you entertain the thought of joy at seeing her? Why would you allow the desire to overcome your senses? Why would you permit the past to enter the present?" she speaks.

She allows several minutes to pass. With her focus on the meeting, the Pathfinder drives away.

Returning to her apartment, Chloe allows a hot shower to drizzle over her pale complexion. The water drips from her forehead. She sits in anger and hurt. The long, hot shower flows into cold as she finally bathes. With a towel wrapped around her, she enters the bedroom to find a note on her bed. She smiles thinking it is from Craig. Her dry fingers retrieve the note carrying it into the kitchen. Chloe glances at the stainless- steel wall clock and remarks out loud, "Omg, I have been in there an hour!"

Her blue eyes change their glance into a glare as she notices the espresso machine brewing a cup. Recalling the last- time the machine was brewing, she is appreciative of Craig's gesture. As she fills her favorite yellow mug, she smiles as the future come to mind. Her mood lightens as the wedding comes to mind. The foam rests atop the steamy cup. She leans against the island blowing into the cup as the foam recedes. "Oh," she comments as the note comes to mind. Her fingers quickly open it.

My dearest Chloe,

I was terribly wrong. I am about to plead for something I have only done one other time. As Megan lay dying in the car, I continuously asked for forgiveness. All I could do was watch as her screams for help filled the night. So, with that same pain and heartache I am asking for your forgiveness. Andrea

Andrea's words echo in her thoughts as she begins to cry. Chloe takes the espresso into her bedroom and places it on the night stand as she looks out into the darkening southeast.

"Chloe, how can you love one and desire another? This has to stop!" she says to herself as Mount Hood is smothered in the darkness. She takes another sip before dressing for the meeting. Forty-five minutes later, Chloe completes her attire by slipping into her black heels. With the briefcase in hand, she locks the door behind herself. Her heels tap the marble as the elevator awaits at the end of the hall. She rides the elevator to the parking garage. She is greeted by a white limousine as she exits the elevator. As she passes the white limousine, the window lowers.

"Chloe, can we talk?" the slightly gruff voice asks.

"No! I have a meeting starting in a half-hour and I need to remain focused," Chloe answers as she continues to her Pathfinder.

"Henry, stop the car!" Andrea demands as she jumps to her feet.

She pursues Chloe until they reach the silver Pathfinder. Reaching over Chloe's shoulder, Andrea pushes the door shut. Chloe lowers her head as frustration and exhaustion enter her athletic body. Andrea places her scarred left hand on Chloe's. Chloe raises her head to notice Andrea's reflection in the window.

"What do you want from me? Please stop! I cannot do this! I have my future to think about!" Chloe says as her hand joins Andrea's at her waist.

"I have only begun. I cannot stop how I feel," Andrea says as her sweet breath rests on Chloe's ear.

"You have to. I love Craig!" Chloe comments as she turns to face Andrea.

"It must be hard to love two people at the same time. I have only been in love once and I still am," Andrea says as she backs away.

Chloe stares into Andrea's shallowing brown eyes.

"You look tired! You need to rest and mourn your mother's passing. Everything else can wait," Chloe says as she caresses Andrea's cheek.

"I have a red-eye Sunday. A client in New York is needing assistance. Can we meet tomorrow?" Andrea asks.

"I don't know? Craig has a flight to Seattle in the morning. I need to think about it," Chloe says giving Andrea hope.

"Please take this and call if you want to," Andrea says handing Chloe her business card before walking away.

The limousine leaves ahead of the Pathfinder.

Chapter Sixteen

The Pathfinder switches lanes as it races toward city hall. A chill freezes Chloe's nerves as she approaches the stone pillars. She shrugs the chill off as she walks through the warm halls. She is greeted by Mr. Griffin at the doors.

"Good evening, Mr. Griffin. Where is our client?" she speaks.

"He will be here shortly," the black-rimmed, slender man answers.

"Good," she says as her eyes show a sign of nervousness.

"Is this the first time you have stood before the council?" he asks holding a briefcase.

"Yes, does it show?" she asks noticing his calm demeanor.

"A little. Just remember to speak when spoken to. Remember, Mr. Waylon has done this a dozen times. He is very impressed with your abilities," the representative comments.

From behind, a hefty man approaches.

"Good evening, Mr. Waylon," Mr. Griffin says with an outstretched hand.

"Good evening, Mr. Griffin. And you must be Miss Conners?" the well-dressed man says offering her his hand.

"It is nice to finally meet you. I have seen your plans for the restaurant. I am happy to see the landmark being restored and not turned into a parking lot," she remarks.

"Call me Bruce. My company buys a handful of these landmarks every year and restores them," he says.

"We should be going inside. The meeting is about to begin," Mr. Griffin instructs.

The room is packed with a variety of people. The three of them find seats in the middle and await their turn.

"What number is our agenda?" Mr. Waylon asks.

"1919, so we might as well relax," Arnie Griffin answers.

"The first agenda is called. We are ready to hear agenda 1915," the mayor says.

"Well, at least there is only four ahead of us," Chloe says.

Two hours later, their case is the last to be heard.

"Good evening, Miss Conners. Are you prepared?" the mayor asks.

Her eyes take notice of his name plate before she answers.

"Yes, Mayor Parker, I am ready. In the individual packets each of you are being handed are a business plan, a miniature scale drawing of the restoration, and the completed project," she states standing at the podium.

"First, is your client here?" the mayor asks as arrogance arrives in his tone.

"Yes, Mayor, he is right here. This is Mr. Waylon," Chloe says as she looks to her left.

"Good, then you did listen," he remarks.

Taken back by his tone, she glances at her client.

"We have two other offers for the same property. One offer wants to make this a parking garage. The other wants to make an apartment complex. Why should we choose your offer over the others?" Councilwoman Reed asks.

"Because mine will maintain the historical value," her client answers as he stands.

"Would you be willing to increase your offer if necessary?" the mayor asks in his deep raspy voice.

"Yes, if it is necessary," Bruce Waylon replies.

"Very well, let us review the files and we will have a decision late next week," Mayor Parker states before adjourning the meeting.

"Thank you, Mayor, for this opportunity," Chloe says as the gavel lowers.

As the meeting ends, Chloe inquiries into the late dinner.

"Are we still on for a late dinner?"

"I am in the mood for a burger," her client remarks.

"Good! I know the perfect spot," Chloe says as a woman with a scarf on her head brushes her arm. Her phone beeps as they walk out.

"Do you mind if my fiancé joins us?" she asks waiting to reply to his text message.

"Not a problem," Mr. Griffin answers.

She sends the location and leads them to her Pathfinder.

The SUV sprays water from tires as the street splatters beneath. The restaurant is a few blocks away. As she pulls into the lot, her client notices the advertisement on the side of the brick building.

"Wow, that is simple yet amazing!"

Chloe steps back and is amazed at the new mural.

"That is different. I love the talent of these artists. I sometimes think it is shameful how such artistry will go unappreciated," she states.

"Why is that?" Mr. Griffins asks.

"Because so many of these graffiti artists will go unnoticed," her client remarks.

Their appreciation ends as the rain begins once more.

The waitress shows them to their table. The rectangle, industrial metal, high top table greets them. The chairs are made with industrial metal. The seat and back have a vinyl cushion.

"Wow, this place is incredible!" her client remarks.

"Wait until you taste the burgers," Chloe states.

She notices Craig entering.

"Excuse me," she says.

Her quick steps reach his welcoming arms. She introduces them as he takes a seat.

"So, how did the meeting go?"

"Well, I am not sure," Chloe says.

"I think next week may be interesting," Mr. Griffin states.

"Really? Why?" Craig asks as Chloe delves into the menu.

"Because the business plan is solid," he states.

The waitress takes their orders and leaves as the conversation drifts from topic to topic.

The thunder applauds as their plates arrive. She is momentarily distracted while placing the napkin on her lap. Familiar legs walk by as she raises her head. Her attention is on Craig's hand resting on her knee. She removes his hand as she redirects her attention to the client. A look of bewilderment crosses his round boyish face. His sandy brown hair and green eyes highlight his former college football days. He notices her focus strengthen as her client talks about his other restorations.

"So, I have never been to Wisconsin. What is the state like?" Craig asks.

Chloe smiles at her fiancé as he inquires. Her smile is interrupted at the sight of Andrea and three others at a table behind them. Her eyes immediately drop to Andrea's well-defined legs.

"Hey, where are you?" Craig asks as his question goes unanswered.

"Sorry, I saw something drop and it caught my attention," Chloe says shaking her head.

"I was talking about our wedding," he says.

"Yes, but I am listed as single for a couple more weeks," she exclaims with a smile.

Throughout dinner, Chloe's glances toward Andrea are not returned.

Their conversation stalls as the ten o'clock hour arrives.

"Well, it is getting late and I have an early flight," Craig says.

"It has been really nice meeting the two of you," Bruce states as his napkin is placed on the table.

As they leave their seats, Chloe shakes their hands. Craig walks ahead talking football with the guys. She shoots Andrea a smile as she leaves. Chloe stops once more to see Andrea rising from her seat. Andrea stares as she catches Chloe watching her. Chloe continues.

She meets her guest at the Pathfinder.

"Where are you staying?"

"We're staying at the Best Western by the airport," Mr. Griffin answers.

Her client and Mr. Griffin step into the SUV as Craig approaches.

"Are we on for a night cap?" he says placing his hands on her waist.

"You need to get some rest. I will pick you up at six!" she says rejecting his offer for intimacy.

"Okay, see you at six," he comments before they kiss.

The temperature slips as the Pathfinder passes the historic district.

"I have a feeling next week is going to be tough," Bruce says adjusting his seatbelt.

"What makes you say that?" Chloe asks as she turns the blinker on.

"Just a feeling. Baltimore is going to be a mess. Most of the members on the council are on the take. So, that means more money or walking away," he says as experience soaks in.

"How do you know this?" she asks as the hotel comes into sight.

"Past experience," he answers. Meanwhile, Mr. Griffin is quietly observing them.

"Well, we're here," she states.

"Mr. Waylon, I am pleased to have met you. Will you be here next week?" she asks.

"No, there is no need for my appearance," he says.

"What are you willing to raise your offer to?" Chloe asks as he reaches for the handle.

"Arnie will let you know. Have a good night, Miss Conners." Her passengers exit.

Chapter Seventeen

After seeing Andrea twenty feet away and Craig sitting next to her, Chloe acknowledges the struggle within. She returns home to her solitude. The SUV seemed to have a homing device for she does not recall the drive. She notices the engagement ring as she opens the door to her apartment. Her favorite merlot is chilled and waiting to help with the decision she is needing to make. As her heels rest on the mat inside the door, she undresses in the other room. She slips a long, silk, eggshell negligée over her warm body. Switching the lamp off and turning the volume down, Chloe allows the night to absorb her thoughts. With the classical music covering the walls, she rests in her high back tapestry chair facing the blackened skies. The merlot swirls as her thoughts deepen. She remembers the first- time meeting Craig. His family had just moved back from New Jersey. Heather was home for the weekend. Heather and Craig are cousins. Craig is a couple years younger than Chloe. He was infatuated at first sight. She was not. Her first thoughts were that of a player. They were at a party and he was flirting with every blonde in the room. She dismissed his attempts at flirting. Over the next couple of years, they grew closer. She awoke next to him one morning and realized her feelings. He was charming and considerate. He made her his world. She allowed him in. She had not done that since Andrea.

He was patient in the beginning. She could not ask for more. As time went on, their relationship became stronger. She had not given Andrea a second thought in three years. It was not until the Supreme Court ruled in favor of gay marriage. The ruling was a gab session among some of the older secretaries. She would be bombarded with requests of her views of the ruling. Chloe would avoid the request by changing the subject or avoiding the gossip. She would find herself wondering if Andrea had celebrated the decision. Chloe would notice women openly holding hands and showing their affections. There were times when she could see herself and Andrea walking together. Chloe often wondered how Andrea was. She has often recalled the night on the dock with regret when she didn't look back. She knew the tears Andrea was forming would stop her. The agony of the last day of camp nearly ripped her heart out. Even though she denied her feelings, Chloe would watch Andrea as she passed by. Heather and her crew would laugh as Andrea sat alone. Their cruel teenager malice did not affect Andrea or, so it seemed. She withstood their barrage of comments. All Chloe could do was wallow in weakness as Andrea's strength endured. The warm August day still resides in her memories. She was passing Andrea's cabin. Her desire stopped her as she saw Andrea leaning against the cot. Chloe stood staring as Andrea finally showed weakness. As Chloe entered, Andrea looked up with tears in her eyes. She always stood when Chloe approached.

"Are you okay?" Chloe asked wanting to hug her.

"Why do you care? Your friends' malicious behavior did not cause you concern, so why are you asking now?" Andrea angrily asks.

"Because I am weak," Chloe states.

"My grandmother just passed. You know how I found out?" Andrea asks.

Chloe shakes her head.

"My father called. They are not coming to get me. I was told to find my own way home. No Chloe, I am not okay! Because I have no way to go home and there is no one to call!" Andrea shouts.

Chloe begins to walk to her but is distracted by Heather.

"I'm coming!" Chloe says before touching Andrea's arm.

Andrea touched her hand, before Chloe stepped away.

Now she realizes the decision she must make. It will either destroy Craig, her family, friends and career. Or she will break the same person's heart again. Knowing how rare second chances are, Chloe sits pondering the life-changing decision. Her merlot warms, and the goosebumps appear as a chill overcomes her. Chloe turns down the satin sheets and retires.

Her slender body begs for rest, but her mind has other ideas. She remembers Andrea's business card. She retrieves it from her briefcase. She pours another glass of merlot. The cold hardwood suggests a hot bubble bath. She places the card and phone on the shelf as she turns the water on. As the steam rises, she pours the milk and honey bubble bath into the rising water. She dips one foot at a time in the hot water and the bubbles form. Lowering herself into the hot welcoming bath, she allows the bubbles to hide her small breast. She enters Andrea's number into her phone and saves it. With the water resting at her neckline, Chloe ponders how to reach out to her. Taking a sip of Merlot, she decides on a text.

"Sorry to text so late."

Silence fills her anticipation of a response.

"Hello, didn't think you would text. How was the meeting?" Andrea replies.

"It went well. Won't know anything until next week. How was your dinner?"

"Meeting went well! Was that Craig next to you?" Andrea quickly asks.

"Yes."

"He is handsome! Too bad I bat for the other team or I would pursue him!" Andrea teases.

"Don't know about the 'too bad batting for the other team,' but that would be one hell of a competition!"

"That would be a mess. Can you imagine that battle? OMG! Portland would go up in flames!" Andrea says.

"Hell, with Portland! We'd kill one another! What are you doing tomorrow?" Chloe finally asks.

"Waiting at the airport now. Wasn't sure I'd hear from you, so I changed my flight," Andrea replies.

Chloe's smile leaves as her anticipation is crushed.

"Sorry, should have text earlier."

"No problem. I do not know if or when I will return to Portland. You would have been my only reason other than Erma, after mom passed," Andrea says baiting a response.

"Did you finally mend the past with her?"

"Yes, it took a long while. Now I have the guilt to live with," she states.

"Erma told me about the crash and the subsequent actions of your parents."

A long pause has Chloe thinking she crossed a line again.

"Thank you, but Megan's pleas haunt me every day," Andrea replies.

"I am sorry! How many times have you heard that?"

"It seems more often lately," Andrea says. "I have to go. My flight is being called!" she writes quickly.

"If I had asked you to spend the day with me, would you have?" Chloe finally gives in to her desire to see Andrea. "Sorry, I wish I would have text sooner. I would have liked spending some time with you without arguing," Chloe says without giving Andrea a chance to answer her previous question.

The decision is about to be made for her as she cries. She has missed the second chance and knows a third is out of reach. She remains lost in emotion as the bubbles dissipate.

Chloe rises well before dawn to drop Craig off. She returns home and back to sleep. The morning arrives waking her a couple hours later. The sunlight awakens her before the alarm. Once more her routine kicks in. She is greeted with the espresso maker brewing her favorite. Sipping on the vanilla latte, her thoughts recall the last two times this has happened. She remembers how Craig was surprised by her gratitude for the latte.

"Wait a minute! Why in the hell would he drive over here make the latte and drive home only to have me pick him up?" Chloe is lost in intrigue as she recalls the note yesterday. "I am confused!" Her thoughts become wild.

Her running shoes squeak as they step toward the elevator. She is met by her neighbor Edith Smith.

"Hello Mrs. Smith, how are you?" Chloe asks as sipping on the cup.

"Hello, my dear, how is your coffee?" her aging voice utters.

"Very good, thank you," Chloe shows gratitude as she thinks her longtime neighbor made the latte.

The early morning damp air greets Chloe as she reaches the parking garage. She notices a new car parked across from her Nissan. It is a charcoal-colored Jaguar. She assumes it belongs to her new neighbor since it is parked in the row her floor is assigned. Her phone beeps before reaching the Pathfinder.

"Good morning, is the offer still standing?" Andrea texts.

"Yeah, but I think New York is a long way to go for a date," Chloe says cheerfully.

"Just a little bit, but how about Portland?" Andrea says followed by a smiley emoji.

"I thought you flew out last night?" Chloe says with shock.

"You asked me to spend the day with you, but you did not give me a chance to answer. So, after I exchanged my ticket, it was late, so I let you sleep. So, what kind of day did you have in mind?" Andrea asks.

"Where are you?" Chloe asks.

"Right behind you!" Andrea texts.

Chloe smiles before turning around. Their eyes lock on and desire melts the moment.

Andrea approaches welcoming Chloe with open arms.

"This is a first! So, what do you want to do?" Chloe asks as her body tingles with anticipation.

"Sauvie Island. I have not been there in a few years," Andrea says walking to Chloe's Pathfinder.

"Really? I did not take you as a bird person," Chloe says unlocking the doors.

"Well, I guess there is a lot we do not know about each other. So, is this a date as you said it was?" Andrea says staring at Chloe's profile.

"We're friends!" Chloe says downplaying the moment.

"So, we're friends on our first date?" Andrea says ribbing Chloe.

"I am not going there," Chloe remarks knowing the conversation is only going downhill.

The SUV leaves the garage. Andrea looks at her phone.

"Who's the message from?" Chloe asks as the Pathfinder rolls to a stop.

"It is from Ridley. She says the jury came back late last night," Andrea answers as she continues to read.

"Is that good or bad?" Chloe asks as she has little experience with the courtroom.

"Well, according to Ridley, the verdict was handed down a half an hour ago. Our client was found guilty!" Andrea says shutting her phone off.

"I'm sorry!" Chloe says.

"Thanks, but she had little to work with. He killed his family and the evidence proved it. Now she will file an appeal and it will be denied. Then she will work on the sentencing hearing and try to plea for his life!" Andrea answers looking at Chloe.

"How do you know the appeal will be denied?" Chloe asks as the SUV continues to Highway 30.

"The prosecution actually did their job. She did not have much to work with to mount an effective defense. Sometimes this just happens. Our client had accepted the reality well before the trial began," Andrea states as Chloe enters a gas station.

"Sorry," she says as Andrea tucks her phone away.

"Are you hungry?" Andrea says noticing the donut sign in the window.

"Yes, make sure you grab some jerky, trail mix, six waters, chips and whatever else you want," Chloe states removing the handle from the gas pump.

"Good lord, are you expecting to work up an appetite?" Andrea says walking away.

Ten minutes later, the passenger door opens, and Andrea tosses two bags onto the back seat.

"What the heck took so long?" Chloe asks looking at her.

"I was being flirted with. She was younger, but cute!" Andrea says baiting a response.

"Where is she?" Chloe asks knowing her question just opened a line of dialect.

"Why do you want to know?" Andrea instantly pounces on the question.

"Damn it!" Chloe remarks knowing Andrea baited her.

"Just kidding, I could not decide on the chips!" Andrea says laughing at Chloe.

"You said it has been a few years since the last visit to Sauvie? Was that the time you saw me in the restaurant?" Chloe asks putting Andrea on the spot.

The Pathfinder enters the traffic.

"Yes," Andrea answers.

"Were you stalking me?" Chloe inquires as the SUV enters Highway 30.

"No. That was fate. I was meeting a client for dinner. Do remember the stare?" Andrea asks hoping Chloe does.

"Yes. Do you realize Craig did not realize our stare? He is so self-absorbed," Chloe says glancing at Andrea.

"I know someone else just like that," Andrea says fumbling through one of the bags.

Chloe smiles at the jab.

"What are you looking for?" she asks noticing Andrea's thumb ring. (It is a steel titanium ring with a rainbow circling it.)

"The donuts!" she says finally finding them. Andrea opens the tabs on the bag of donuts.

"Are those the chocolate ones?" Chloe asks glancing at the bag.

"Yep, you want one?" Andrea offers.

"Yes, but Craig would frown on it. He says they will make me fat," Chloe says trying to refrain from accepting one.

"Well, I am not him and believe me you look amazing!" Andrea says referring to her figure.

"Thank you. Can I have one?" Chloe asks.

"Yep, open and say yum," Andrea says.

As the mile marker passes, Chloe opens wide and Andrea places a donut on her tongue.

Chapter Eighteen

A few miles later and the SUV turns onto Sauvie Island Bridge.

"I have missed the island. My father would bring us here on the weekends," Andrea says as the SUV turns left.

"My parents were always busy building the business. The restaurant was their focal point," Chloe comments.

"When was the first time you ever came here?" Andrea asks closing the tabs on the bag.

"Just now," she says looking around.

"Are you kidding me?" Andrea says realizing this is another first.

"Wow, another first for us?" Chloe says hiding her childhood regret.

"You want get out?" Andrea asks trying to deflect Chloe's sadness.

The SUV exits onto a pull-off. Reading Chloe's emotions, Andrea turns in her seat facing Chloe. Taking Chloe's hand, Andrea's heart races. They sit in silence for fear of what could be next.

"Where do you want to go?" Chloe asks leaving her hand in Andrea's.

"Look at me, please?" Andrea says.

In doing so, Chloe allows her tears to fall.

"What is this about?" Andrea asks as cars pass by.

"What a turn! Your parents had time for family getaways and mine did not," Chloe answers.

"Hey, don't go there. At least your parents wanted you," Andrea says taking the hurt Chloe is feeling onto herself.

Chloe looks up to notice Andrea offering her a water.

"Why do you always try to take my pain away?" Chloe asks twisting the cap off.

"You know why! So, let's stop this line before we begin to argue," Andrea says releasing her hand and opening the door.

Chloe packs the snacks into a backpack she had laying in the back and hands it to Andrea. As they begin their hike, Chloe watches Andrea's eyes dance with excitement.

The wide path affords them walking side by side. The leaves swing on the breeze as they pass a bench.

"Hey, let's have a seat for a second," Chloe says when the sun patches through the trees.

Andrea takes the suggestion and sits next to her.

"At the hardware store, you said you were no longer seeing someone. Was the someone a serious relationship?" Chloe inquires wanting a deep personal conversation.

"Yes. I have only had one serious relationship since our teenage years," Andrea openly answers.

Chloe allows her answer to sink in.

"Why did you ask me to spend the day with you?" Andrea asks.

"Because I needed to know that we could have a civil conversation without the petty arguments. Plus, I just wanted to be me for change. Instead of what others want me to be. You are the only one I have ever been that with," Chloe says taking Andrea by surprise.

The leaves rustle as a creek trickles below. Chloe releases the hold and walks to the railing in front of them. Removing her phone, Andrea snaps a picture of Chloe staring at the water.

"What are you doing looking at your messages? I thought this was a date?" Chloe says breaking the moment with humor.

"Just making sure you are paying attention. So, this is a date?" Andrea says standing to continue their hike.

"Yeah, right! I am not going to answer the date question," Chloe states walking by her.

Andrea grins at her reply as she follows.

The path continues to wind past gullies and ravines. The sun blotches their trail as the dirt path sinks beneath them. Andrea reaches in the backpack. Her hand twists the cap off and takes a drink while waiting for Chloe to catch up. With her phone in hand, Andrea snaps a photo of the path.

"Hey, did I just catch you on your phone again?" Chloe says stopping in front of her to take several deep breathes.

"Nope, I was taking pictures. Here," Andrea says offering her a water.

With Chloe drinking several swallows, Andrea decides to test the water. She places her hand on Chloe's hip. Her test was not rejected as Chloe left Andrea's hand on her. Chloe's heart pounds with the sensation of Andrea touching her. She does not react to the familiar hand. Stepping away from her hand, Chloe continues the hike.

The path continues to twist them deeper into the woods. Seeing a table, Chloe comments,

"Hey, let's stop and rest. I am kind of hungry!"

Andrea smiles as an idea comes to mind.

"Don't you even think about it. I remember the table at camp," Chloe says recalling their star gazing when they were eighteen.

Andrea smiles knowing Chloe was thinking the same. Chloe takes the side facing a thicket with a ravine flowing below. Andrea places one leg over the seat and begins to raise the other.

"Nope, sit on the other side!" Chloe commands.

"Why? I don't want to just stare at the rocks behind you," Andrea says trying to bait her.

"You know why! So, sit on the other side!" Chloe says.

"Screw that! You can sit over there!" Andrea says dropping the backpack on the table.

Chloe rises and begins to step over the weathered bench seat.

"Clo, please just sit there and we will talk. I promise not to cross any lines. I just want to talk!" Andrea pleads placing her sore hand on Chloe's forearm.

"Tell me how you and Craig met?" Andrea asks as she opens the bag of pretzels.

"Well, he is Heather's cousin. She introduced us and that is pretty much the whole story," Chloe says reaching into the offered bag.

Glancing at the bruises on Chloe's wrist, Andrea continues to delve.

"So, is he romantic? Does he satisfy you? Is he good to you?" Andrea runs questions together.

"No, none of your business, and for the most part," Chloe swiftly answers.

"Why is he not romantic?" Andrea asks chomping on a pretzel.

Passing the bag to Chloe, their hands touch.

"Thank you," Chloe says grabbing a handful of mini pretzels and returning the bag to her hiking buddy.

"You are welcome. So please continue," Andrea says drinking in the beauty of Chloe's profile.

"Because he is always busy and doesn't have time for that," Chloe frankly responds.

"I call bullshit! He is no busier than me. If I were him, you would be romanced every day!" Andrea says flirting with her love.

"Thank you for that," she says grabbing a bottle.

"So, none of my business when it comes to the satisfying question, huh?" Andrea asks knowing a comment is coming.

"Why do you want to know?" Chloe throws the question back with a crooked smile.

"Because this is what women talk about. Besides, I want to know how high the bar is he has set. I just want to know if I could ever match it," Andrea says touching her hand.

"Dre, please stop," Chloe says with a grin.

"Will you please turn and face me? I would appreciate it if you would," Andrea says dispensing with all flirtatious tone.

She hesitates, knowing the stare awaiting her.

"Chloe, please?" Andrea now begs.

Turning to face Andrea, Chloe bends her knee across the seat. Andrea tosses the pretzel bag on the table and moves closer.

"Now, look at me and listen very closely. I was so surprised at how beautiful you were sitting in the train station. I was taken back. I have loved you at first sight and nothing has changed sitting here eight years later. In my heart you will always be my only true love. But, time has different ideas. So, now I sit here staring at the only person I will ever be in love with. Believe me, I hear you loud and clear when you say there is no us. I also hear you when you say we were just an escapade of youth. That hurts, but I only want you to be happy. That is why I asked if he is good to you," Andrea says touching her thigh.

Removing her hand, Andrea steps over the bench and carries on along the path carrying the backpack.

Chloe remains temporarily behind to allow her tears to dry.

"God, I love her. I just wish things were different," Chloe says looking toward the bright blue sky.

The final leg of their trail comes in view. Chloe smiles at the incline and grins at Andrea.

"What are you grinning at?" Andrea says noticing the peace in her smile.

"Can you make it to the top before me?" Chloe says pointing at the steep climb.

Standing in front of Andrea, Chloe does so hoping Andrea will return her hand to her hip. Andrea does not disappoint. Her scarred hand rests on her hip.

"Don't worry, I like being on top," Andrea smirks at Chloe's dumbfounded look.

"Well so do I!" Chloe says teasing her.

Chloe watches as Andrea walks on. She has never teased anyone the way she has Andrea. Chloe suddenly dashes past Andrea to make it to the top first.

"Told you I like being on top!" Chloe says leaning against the boulders.

"Yes, but can you stay there! Believe me, most end up on the bottom," Andrea says returning the provocation.

Chloe leans against the boulders catching her breath.

"Now see, you worked those donuts off," Andrea remarks taking deep breaths.

Chloe smiles as her phone beeps. She glances at the message. Her eyes deepen as Andrea assumes to know the sender.

"Do you need to end our day?" Andrea asks thinking Craig is texting.

"No, it's my Mom. She wants to meet tomorrow," Chloe says not telling Andrea everything.

"So, where to now?" Andrea asks cheering on the inside.

Chloe walks up to Andrea and kisses her. The passion consumes them as Chloe walks her against the boulders. Their lips moisten each other as the wind swirls the cul-de-sac. Andrea slowly unzips Chloe's bubble vest untucking her plaid long sleeve shirt, allowing her hands to slip around Chloe's waist.

"Not here!" Chloe says stopping her hands from advancing. She leads Andrea back to the SUV.

The forty-minute hike is shortened by Chloe's desire. She practically drags Andrea behind. Then the Pathfinder comes in view. Andrea returns to the passenger seat. Chloe climbs on Andrea's lap pulling the door shut. Andrea's hands resume their previous position. Chloe leans in and they begin to kiss once more. Unbuttoning her own shirt, Chloe then reaches between the seat and door lowering Andrea's seat after speaking.

"Take your shirt off!" she demands of Andrea.

Her blue eyes notice scarring on Andrea's well-endowed, deeply tanned chest. The passion and desire pull her attention from the scars. Andrea frees Chloe's belt from the buckle allowing the button to be loosened. Chloe looks down and smiles. She begins to speak. Her words are halted by Andrea's lips. With the seat reclined, Chloe rests her breast against Andrea's. Her fingers are the culprit for Chloe's moan. Chloe drives her hips forward onto Andrea's long filling fingers. Andrea pushes her will with every movement of Chloe's hips. Arching her blonde head for the third time, Chloe collapses onto Andrea's chest. Finally, Chloe rises to disengage from the moment. Andrea breathes heavily as Chloe steps from the vehicle.

With her jeans unbuttoned and shirt open, Chloe leans against the SUV.

"Oh my god!" she says with disbelief at her actions.

Raising her seat, Andrea steps from the vehicle and remarks, "I did not see that coming!"

"I cannot believe I did that!" Chloe says zipping her jeans.

"Are you okay?" Andrea asks noticing Chloe is rubbing her belly.

"Yes, it has been awhile since I had multiples!" Chloe says stepping around Andrea to retrieve the hand sanitizer from her console.

"Really? Like how long?" Andrea asks feeling gratified in her abilities.

"Eight years," Chloe says stepping around Andrea.

"Here!" she hands Andrea the trial size bottle before answering her phone.

"Hello? Hi Mom. Sorry your message just came through. Nope, I can't. I have plans tonight. I will see you in the morning. Love you too," Chloe says looking at Andrea.

"You have plans tonight?" Andrea says rubbing the sanitizer on her hand.

"Yes, now that the sexual frustration is over! Would you like to have lunch?" Chloe says turning around.

"Sure," Andrea answer placing her hand on Chloe's fit waist.

They kiss before Chloe walks to the driver's side with a wide smile and gleaming eyes.

As they head south on Interstate 5 to Salem, Chloe takes her hand.

"So, when do you fly out?"

"My flight leaves at three A.M. on Monday morning. So, what are we going to do?" Andrea responds.

"Well, I thought we could grab a bite and then do some shopping? And later, you can repeat our earlier excursion," Chloe says allowing her flirtation to show.

"I have never seen or thought you would be this flirtatious," Andrea says opening a bottle of water.

"It is because with you I can be. I just don't feel this way with Craig," Chloe all but tells Andrea that she loves her.

"Why are you marrying him?" Andrea asks knowing this is going to spark an argument.

"Please, let's not mention him. You just gave me three orgasms in a public place and now we're headed for lunch!" Chloe says stopping the conversation.

Andrea notices Chloe's bruised wrists once more as she removes her hand.

"What happened to your wrist?" Andrea asks.

"I was carrying a file box to my office yesterday and it slipped down my arm.

"Ouch! That happened often when I was a paralegal! I do not miss those days," Andrea says looking out.

"Me neither. What is it like to be a trial lawyer?" Chloe asks.

"Scary at first, but like everything else, practice makes you a pro. I remember the first time I second chaired. I was scared to death," Andrea explains.

"What is the scariest part?" Chloe asks switching lanes.

"I think the closing. Because the opening is simply an explanation of what you plan to do. The trial is showing what you are doing. But the closing is for me, because it is your last chance to sway twelve people's opinions," Andrea says.

"I know contract is not as glamorous, but I still get goosebumps with new clients," Chloe says.

"I could not imagine writing up a contract that may very well change someone's future," Andrea says.

"Yeah, but with trial, are you not affecting someone's life?" Chloe states.

"Perhaps, but the type of people I represent usually deserve a guilty plea," Andrea says looking at her phone.

"Have you ever represented an innocent person?" Chloe asks as they reach the turnoff.

"Not that I know of," Andrea answers.

"Is everything okay?" Chloe inquires as she notices Andrea's intense glare at her message.

"Yes, my client's father will meet me at La Guardia on Monday," Andrea says as the Pathfinder enters Salem.

"Oh man, I could not tell you the last time I was in Salem. I am thinking I was barely a teenager," Andrea says looking at how much the city has grown.

"I come here a handful times a year. I love this little diner I am taking you to," Chloe says trying to show Andrea a different side.

The small greasy spoon has an old-world charm. The restaurant is two blocks off the main street. It is a white brick building with a hut style roof.

"Here we go," Chloe says.

"I love the whole quaint feeling already," Andrea says looking at roof.

Chloe smiles before reaching for Andrea's chin turning it to look in those brown eyes she felt so safe with long ago.

"Hi," is the only word Chloe says before kissing Andrea hard on her thin lips.

"Hey," Andrea replies just before separating her lips to allow Chloe's tongue entryway.

"Shit!" Chloe exclaims pulling away.

Andrea smiles at her word choice. Chloe smiles back reaching for the door handle.

As they enter the small family diner, Chloe is greeted.

"Well, hello Chloe, how are you?" the young man asks.

"Hello, Domingo, I am fine and how are you and the family?" she says shaking his hand.

"We are all fine," he says leading them to a table.

"This is Andrea. She is a longtime friend of mine," Chloe says as Andrea offers her hand to him.

Andrea excuses herself to use the restroom. She returns momentarily to a hunger stare from Chloe. The waiter approaches. He places the menu in front of them and leaves. While Andrea looks over the menu, Chloe rubs Andrea's leg with her foot. With the afternoon arriving, Chloe makes a bold statement.

"Would you make love to me if we go back to my apartment?"

Taken back by her forthcoming, Andrea only nods at her request. As their lunch arrives, Chloe begins her inquisitive nature.

"So, what made you choose criminal law?"

"Please do not take this the wrong way, but my days of being bullied carved the desire to help those in need," Andrea answers slicing her chicken.

"There is no other way to take that. I am sorry for what you went through. I should have been stronger," she replies.

"That's okay. I was battered but not broken. Besides, at least I found love through the whole thing," Andrea says adding butter to her baked potato.

Chloe stares at her strong jaw line and saddens on the inside. "I want to cry when I think about what we did to you! Yet, I am also very enamored with your resolve," Chloe says touching her hand.

"Why? I am just someone who survived a bad situation and was able to rise above things. This does not make me any more special than anyone else," Andrea says watching Chloe pepper her fried potatoes.

"But you are to me," Chloe says revealing her feeling to Andrea.

"You know I simply love our petty arguments. I like how we get to each other," Andrea says trying to lighten the moment.

"Do you remember what we argued about on the third day on the first go-around at camp?" Chloe asks smiling.

"I am sure it was something petty. Give me a second," Andrea says. Chloe studies her facial expressions as Andrea drudges for the answer. "Those damn beanbags! You were pissed because my team chose the red colored ones!" Andrea recalls.

"You're right. I was pissed because the red team should have had the red bags. Omg, do you remember the shoving match?" Chloe recalls with a smile.

"Yes, I also remember us covered in mud and throwing the bags at each other," Andrea says laughing at their antics.

"Erma was so pissed at us! Do you remember her scolding us in her office?" Chloe adds.

"Yes, we were sitting in those hard-ass, plastic chairs with mud splattering on the new linoleum. My god, she was so ticked at us!" Andrea says.

"Do you recall the dining hall episode?" Chloe asks as she takes a sip of her water.

"Yes! She was punishing us for the beanbag mess. Why would she think placing us on clean-up duty would have solved anything?" Andrea states before taking a bite.

"I remember getting pissed at you because you refused to take the trash bag out," Chloe says sitting Indian-style.

"Damn it, you were only filling those forty-five-gallon trash bags half-full and I had already taken four out and we hadn't made a dent in the clean up!" Andrea chuckles.

"I was enjoying watching you haul them out. That was until you dumped the next bag on new shoes," Chloe says.

"Then you flung a rotten tomato at me and that was it! The war was on!" Andrea says laughing.

"We had food on every wall and table. That shit was all over!" Chloe says giggling.

"I also remember our expressions when we realized what we had done," Andrea says laughing.

"We had that we-are-so-fucked look. That is when I realized I was having feelings for you," Chloe adds enlightening Andrea.

"I was attracted to you the first night when I challenged you!" Andrea says staring into her eyes.

"That was a long night! What should have taken us two hours ended up taken eight hours. I purposely slowed down. I was enjoying the time alone with you!" Andrea says.

"I know. Why do you think I washed the same wall three times? I also recall walking on the trail back to the cabins after showering. I wanted you to accidently touch my hand," Chloe says revealing her wish to Andrea.

"Why did you slip into the tree line when my gang arrived?" Chloe asks noticing Andrea reverting to silence.

"Because they would have known our desires simply by looking at our stare," Andrea answers.

Placing her hand on Andrea's, Chloe speaks.

"Thank you for protecting me."

"You're welcome," Andrea says with soft eyes.

They continue to laugh well into the afternoon. When Chloe's phone rings, Andrea takes the opportunity to stare into her eyes.

Noticing the caller, Chloe declines to answer. She pays the tab and they head back to Portland.

Chapter Nineteen

The quiet apartment welcomes them. With her shoes landing on the mat next to the door, Chloe locks the door. Andrea follows Chloe's cue by removing her shoes.

"Would you like a drink?" Chloe offers.

"Sure!" Andrea answers before walking to the window. As Andrea looks out the window overlooking the river, Chloe approaches.

"Here you go," she says handing Andrea a drink.

"Thank you," Andrea replies.

Chloe catches Andrea off guard as she lifts her right arm and steps in front of Andrea. Chloe then wraps Andrea's arm around her. Leaning against Andrea, they stare out at the fading day. Andrea gives into the desire to rest her forehead against Chloe's head. A sense of peace and fate comes over Andrea as she allows the future to come to mind. Thirty minutes pass before Chloe speaks.

"Let's go. I want you to make love to me."

They place their drinks on the end table behind them.

She takes Andrea by the hand and runs down the hall. Chloe pulls Andrea on top of her as the pillow top cuffs their fall. Just shy of two hours,

Andrea collapses next to an exhausted Chloe. They lay in silence allowing their bodies to breathe. Turning onto her side, Andrea cuddles with Chloe. The sun's last stance glistens the snowcap on Mount Hood as they lay staring at the view.

"What a view," Andrea says squeezing Chloe.

"Stop talking and just hold me. I need this now," Chloe states.

Chloe just wants the moment to reside on her soul. With a beep of her phone, Chloe grunts.

"Who is it?" Andrea asks.

"Craig," Chloe says releasing Andrea's grip.

"No Chloe, stay here and just be in the moment," Andrea demands wrapping her arm around Chloe.

She pulls Chloe back down next to her. Chloe's eyes close as she pulls the sheet to her shoulder. In this moment, a sense of intimacy cradles Chloe as she relaxes.

"I have never been held before!" Chloe says.

"Not even afterwards?" Andrea asks with astonishment.

"No, he would walk to the shower," she says revealing her apartment life.

"My God, what is wrong with him? This is the most sensual moment. I cannot believe he would not want to hold you. He is a fool!" Andrea boldly claims.

"Thank you," Chloe says with tenderhearted gratitude.

The walls are padded with silence as the calmness fills the air.

The peacefulness rattles as her phone rings once again.

"Damn it!" Chloe says removing Andrea's arm.

She walks to the shower. As the hot water beads on her smooth skin, Chloe cries. Her future just became clouded. Her loyalty to her lie and the life she projects is now muddled with the day's events. She showers quickly. With the steamed door opening, Andrea stands in the doorway watching her.

"Hi," Chloe says with her sweet smile.

"Hi," Andrea returns the comment as Chloe steps from the shower.

"Do you mind if I shower?" Andrea asks.

"Nope, not at all," Chloe says.

She reaches into the bamboo closet handing Andrea a towel set. She places a toothbrush on the counter.

"Thanks," Andrea says stepping into the warm white shower.

Chloe throws on lounge pants and an old t-shirt. She makes her way into the kitchen. Her phone beeps over and over. To her dismay, it is Craig.

"Hello!" she responds.

"Did you get my text about the early morning suggestion?"

"Yes, but I have to meet Mom at eight. No, I have to decline," she says trying to avoid him.

"Damn, I am turned on and you won't even help?"

"No," Chloe answers.

Andrea watches Chloe's frustration from the hall.

With her hair still damp, Andrea joins Chloe as she strokes her hair with a hand towel.

"Thank you for the toothbrush," Andrea says tucking her shirt in.

"Any time," Chloe responds as her phone beeps again.

Taking the phone from her hand, Andrea presses the power button. Sliding her phone across the counter, Andrea kisses Chloe. Chloe readily accepts her lips and offers hers. Andrea slowly pulls her lips away and Chloe begins to cry. With her tears falling, Andrea pulls Chloe into her arms.

"Please do not marry him? It is your touch that has sustained me for these eight long years. I can't keep it together knowing you are laying with him and never me again," Andrea pleads.

Chloe breaks the hold and steps away. Andrea pours herself a whiskey on the rocks.

"Why did you bolt from bed when he texted?" Andrea asks swirling her glass.

"Because, it is disrespectful to you. I was lying next to you while he texts me! All I wanted was to lay there next to you," she answers walking to the table.

Andrea has made a career out of reading people. Chloe is no different. She reads Chloe's changing tone.

"So, what's going on?" Andrea asks sitting across from her.

With her leg tucked under herself, Chloe answers. "I just had one of the best days of my life just being with you and yet it scares me."

"What scares you?" Andrea asks not letting Chloe step away emotionally.

"How perfect it was. We fit together," Chloe says sipping on her merlot.

"Nothing is perfect. We made it perfect by just being two people who have feelings for one another. At least one of us does," Andrea says sensing rejection coming.

"You must know that I love being with you, because I do love you," Chloe says surprising Andrea.

"You love me?" Andrea responds in a question with a smile.

"The moment you stood before me at the train station, those eight years came back. I knew then what I was unwilling to admit. Do you honestly believe I could have done those things today if I wasn't in love with you?" Chloe remarks with a sense of relief at the release of her feelings.

"But," Andrea remarks

"I had created a life and lie for myself. I am not a cold person and you know that, right?" Chloe asks wanting Andrea to answer.

"Yes, of course I know you're not," Andrea reaffirms.

"Please know that I do not know if I am ready or capable of not living a lie. I just don't know if I can do that," Chloe says taking her hand.

"Then that is something you must decide," Andrea says sliding her hand from under Chloe's.

Andrea leaves the table placing her glass on the counter. She leans against the counter momentarily to see Chloe's reaction.

"I have just spent the day with the one person I have longed for my entire life. I do not know if I have another eight years to be lonely while waiting for you. I am not forcing you to decide nor am I angry. You have no idea how lonely and hard this time has been for me," Andrea says walking to the door.

As she slips on her running shoes, Chloe joins her.

"Andrea, please don't be mad. Please do not cry," Chloe begs as her tears form.

A long stare is followed by slow desiring kiss.

"I am not mad. It isn't fair. Please don't break my heart again," Andrea says walking out.

Chapter Twenty

As her Sunday begins, her mother calls.

"Hello Mother, what are you doing up so early?" Chloe asks.

"Hello, I am shocked! My daughter actually answers her phone!" Ruth sarcastically states.

"Good morning to you too," Chloe returns the tone.

"Hey, would you like to participate with your own wedding plans?" Ruth asks.

"I don't know if there is going to be a wedding?" Chloe answers honestly.

"Oh wait, what? No. Get yourself over here this instant!" Ruth demands.

"Mom, I need some time!" Chloe says as she tries to defend her last statement.

"You have thirty minutes!" Ruth says sternly.

"Okay," Chloe says as her mood lightens.

In the meantime, her hand caress the wedding announcement kept in the album beside Chloe's photo.

The Pathfinder drabs it's pace to deflect her mother's demands. Burnside Bridge lays smothered by fog as she crosses it in her path to her parent's. She passes the familiar white picket fence. As she turns onto their road, she spots the neighbors' horses running in the pasture. "I wish I could join you!" she says. Chloe would always run along the fence as the show horses would follow. One of the thoroughbreds would nudge her as she rested against the fence. Chloe would giggle as they played. The hidden driveway was always visible when a scolding was coming. This time it is no different. She slows the pace hoping to prolong the preaching her ears are about to receive. As the Pathfinder reaches the house, Chloe's phone dings. A smile lightens her dim mood.

"Good morning, Chloe," Andrea texts.

"Good morning, Andrea. How are you?"

"I am fine. Did you sleep well?" Andrea inquires.

"Yeah, but a scolding is coming."

"?" is the only reply Andrea has.

"Told Mom not sure a wedding will happen."

"Really?" Andrea exclaims with joy.

"After yesterday, I am not sure what to do! I am not sure he is the one. Or maybe cold feet? Don't truly know."

"Yes, you do! All you have to be honest with yourself," Andrea inserts.

"I wish someday to show you all the places we have been. Regardless of where I was, you were there. I really wish you could see Ellis Island. She is a beauty. Each time I see her, I am reminded of the choices I have made. Just glad to make my own choices and not be pressured into them," Andrea states.

"Maybe someday we can? For now, Mom is pacing. Can I text later?" Chloe asks.

"Sure! Chloe, I love you," Andrea says.

Chloe smiles as the conversation lifts her. "Oh damn, here comes the ass chewing," Chloe remarks as she steps from the Pathfinder.

The cobblestone walk rises from the ground to meet her every step. She barely reaches the door and Heather surprises her.

"OMG, you're here?" Chloe says with joy.

"Oh Clo, I have missed my friend. And what is this I hear? You're not sure about Craig?" Heather says as she escorts Chloe to the kitchen.

"Yeah, something like that," Chloe says with hesitation.

"Well, we have to work on that," Heather says as Ruth walks in.

"Oh look, Heather, she actually shows up," Ruth says enticing as reply.

"Mom, I am not in the mood for sarcasm," Chloe comments as she takes a seat.

"Oh, lighten up, we have a wedding to plan," Ruth states as she flops magazines in front of Chloe.

"Mom, what did I just tell you? I am not sure the wedding will happen," Chloe forcefully states pushing the *Brides* magazines away.

"Oh, come on, you're just having cold feet," Ruth comments.

"Mom, I need some space to relax and clear my head," Chloe begs of her.

"Mrs. Conners, what do you say to the three us spend the day shopping and reminiscing?" Heather interjects.

"Okay, let's have fun!" Ruth says reading Chloe's anger level.

In the meantime, the mayor is fuming at the file he just opened.

"How the hell was this discovered?" he angrily states.

"What are we going to do?" a burly man demands.

"You have to withdraw your offer for the building. We will be left with only two offers," he realizes.

"Why should I lose city money?" the unshaven man remarks.

"You are fucking idiot, because it will look like what it is, a bribe! Do you want a federal investigation or jail?" the irritated mayor answers.

"Fine, I will withdraw the offer," the burly contractor states.

The three ladies arrive downtown to clear skies. Chloe helps her mother from the SUV.

"Oh, by the way, what is up with the ball cap and jeans?" her mother inquires.

"I get tired of suits and heels," Chloe replies as they enter a bridal store. Dampening her aggravation, Chloe enters the shop.

"Chloe, play along for now. We will talk later," Heather advises her.

"Mom, what did you have in mind?" Chloe asks.

"Well, I was thinking classic. And you?" Ruth speaks realizing Chloe is coming around.

"Something short and classy," Chloe adds.

Their shopping lasts for three hours before the right dress is found.

"I told you to play along, not be forced into it!" Heather states.

"I know, but I really liked the dress," Chloe answers.

"Heather, how are the kids?" Chloe asks as they walk to the next store.

"They're fine. The divorce has been hard, but they're adjusting," she says.

"That is good to know. I am so excited my bestie has returned," Chloe says as she wraps her arm around Heather.

"You two knock that off! I do not want anyone thinking you are a couple," Ruth says as she enters the bakery.

Heather smiles like she did when they were children. The coy crooked smile always brought joy to Chloe. Chloe rolls her eyes as she

holds the door for Heather. Heather is two inches shorter than Chloe. Her rustic brown hair has streaks of auburn. Heather has a much more defined, muscular shape than Chloe. Her arms are well-toned with strong, pronounced calves. Her long hair draws the pointed jaw toward her hefty chest. Heather was and still could be a room stopper. She has curvy hips and wheat-tinted eyes with a hue of hay mixed in. Chloe always played second fiddle to her beauty. Heather was the lust of every high schooler. The young guys flocked to her like birds to freshly-tilled soil. Most days Chloe was invisible standing beside Heather. Heather even flirted with the guys Chloe liked. There were many times Chloe would break away from the gang and find solace in the library. She has always loved books. Heather was the opposite. She had no desire in reading. Her parents paid for tutors. Ruth and Ray could not afford Chloe that luxury. Chloe settled for the library and her own determination to succeed.

They sit and taste a dozen cakes.

"Mom, I am not sure I want cake."

The gaze Ruth provided her was priceless.

"Yes, you do, so now decide between these three!" Ruth exclaims.

Chloe's phone rings in time to disrupt an oncoming argument.

"Excuse me," Chloe says as she steps outside.

"Chloe Conners, can I help you?"

"Hello, Miss Conners. I have heard that one of the offers have been withdrawn. I did not mean to disrupt your weekend. I just thought you would like to know," Mr. Griffins states.

"No problem. Thank you for informing me," Chloe says. She is all smiles as the aroma from the bakery tantalizes the air.

"Well, let me guess. That is work and you have to go?" Ruth says.

"Yes, it is work, but no, it can wait," Chloe says as she tries to partake in the tasting.

"Mom, I just am not into this today. Can we do something different?" she asks.

"No, now choose one of these!" Ruth demands of her adult child.

"The yellow is fine. Can we go somewhere else now?" Chloe begs.

"What is wrong with you?" Ruth states as she pays for the cake.

Chloe walks ahead. She leans over the railing near the waterfront. Ruth and Heather join her.

"Now you have two weeks before the wedding and I have done all of the planning.. What is the matter?" Ruth says as she places her hand on Chloe's.

"Mom, you never heard me. I am having second thoughts. I do not know if I even love him any longer," Chloe blurts as her tears and frustration boil.

"Chloe, I think you need to take a break and breathe," Heather adds.

"My child, you are simply having pre-wedding jitters. We have all had them," Ruth says trying to calm her.

"Chloe, do you love him? Do you miss him when the two of you are apart?" Heather asks.

"Yes, but I am not sure he is the one," Chloe defends her position.

"That is love, my dear," Ruth says.

"Besides, we always wanted to be related, right?" Heather says bringing the childhood wishes into the picture.

"Yes, that is right," Chloe agrees.

"So, why don't we get a bite and take a break from the planning?" Heather says playing peacemaker.

Ruth backs off and agrees with a nod. The second half of the day is relaxing for Chloe as their shopping for the wedding is detoured.

As the day ends, the SUV returns its passengers to Ruth's. As the SUV comes to a stop, Chloe's phone beeps. She glances at the messenger. A smile ensues as her passengers step out. She remains behind answering the text.

"Hi back."

"Do you have any ass left?" Andrea asks as she looks at the river.

"Some."

"Good," Andrea answers.

"Let me text you back later," Chloe says as she grins with joy.

"I will talk to you later," Andrea says.

Chloe follows them inside. As they sit around the kitchen table, her father comes in. Her inner smile is for Andrea.

"Well, if it isn't my child. How are you?" he says hugging her.

"I am fine, Papa!" she answers.

"Well, let me tell you what kind of day we have had. Your daughter is having doubts about the wedding. I had to force her to try on the dress and choose the cake!" Ruth snobbishly comments.

"Well, why don't you get off her back? It is not your wedding!" her father Ray states.

Chloe chuckles as he defends her. Heather is speechless at his words.

"Chloe, can you give Heather a ride home?" he asks.

"Yep," she says.

"Have a good night. Your mother and I are about to have a discussion and you are not invited!" he exclaims.

His deep voice becomes loud as the discussion begins. With the house emptying, Ray begins the conversation.

"My dear, why are you so demanding of this wedding?"

"Because they make a perfect couple and the Meagers' would be great in-laws! Why are you not?" she asks.

"Have you seen the bruises on our daughter? No, you haven't, because you're so wrapped up in the thought of the Meagers' that you have forgotten Chloe's happiness!" Ray shouts before walking outside.

The city lights rise from the dimming day as the Pathfinder crosses the bridge.

"So, what made you say you're not sure you still love my cousin?" Heather asks.

"We've been together for so long. I get tired of him being gone every weekend," Chloe says as the SUV switches lanes.

"He is gone every weekend?" Heather questions.

"Nearly!" Chloe says trying to convince her long-time friend of her wavering.

"Have you tried talking to him? Or are you scared of commitment?" Heather asks as she plays counselor.

"Commitment no, just not sure he is the one," Chloe she reiterates.

"What caused the insecurity?" Heather inquires.

"The past few weeks I have been thinking about the past, the future, and where it might take me," Chloe says. Chloe briefly considers explaining her sexuality conflict but soon stops by Heather's next comment.

"Oh please, tell me you're not turning gay. That would destroy your family. I just cannot tolerate seeing two women kissing or touching. That is repulsive!" Heather states as her soapbox is in full gear.

Chloe remains quiet as her best friend snaps.

"What was her name from camp? She was gay. I thought she had a crush on you. Especially the way you were hanging together. The group was getting worried she was turning you. So, we dealt with that!" Heather remarks.

"You can't turn someone gay. What do you mean you dealt with that?" Chloe states as she pulls into the Meagers' residence.

"We noticed the way she would stare at you. So, we dealt with her. Are you becoming sensitive? You are sure not the same Chloe I remember from camp," Heather comments.

"I am the same, just realizing not everything is black and white. What did you do to her?" Chloe demands her position.

"We had several conversations with her before she finally backed off. Are you coming in?" Heather asks.

"Nah, I am going home. Mom just wears on me," Chloe says as they hug.

"We should have a girls' night out. I am sure the gang would love a reunion," Heather says.

"Yes, that would be fun," Chloe states as their embrace ends.

"Later, Chloe. Love you," Heather says as she steps out.

The SUV backs out of the long drive and heads downtown. She decides to stop at a liquor store. Her phone beeps as she pulls into a parking space.

"How did it go today? Can I call?" Andrea texts.

"Okay and yes call," Chloe rapidly responds.

"Hi!" Andrea says with pure joy in her voice.

"Hey, stranger, what have you been up to?" Chloe asks as her smile encroaches.

"Just packing for New York. So, how did it go today?" Andrea asks wanting to hear Chloe's smooth voice.

"Mom was relentless about the wedding. I chose a gown and the damn cake," Chloe says.

"I thought you were having second thoughts?" Andrea says as her cheerfulness recedes, and her tears begin.

"I am. Just covering my bases," Chloe says leaning against her SUV.

"What does that mean?" Andrea says as she falls to the sofa in her apartment.

"I am so confused! I don't know what to do," Chloe says hoping for pity.

"Yeah, it must suck being in love with two people. Especially when only one is honest!" Andrea angrily replies.

"What does that mean?"

"When is the wedding?" Andrea asks.

"On the fifteenth. Why?" Chloe asks.

"Has anyone told you how self-centered you are?" Andrea comments.

"WTF is wrong with you?" Chloe asks instigating an argument.

"Nothing. Wait, I take that back. We just had sex twice and multiples orgasms! You know my feelings for you and how long I have had them, yet you have no qualms about crushing them! I cannot do this anymore! It is my turn to say goodbye. I hope someday you will know how heartbroken I am. I have loved you all my life and always will. Goodbye Chloe," her gruff voice turns raspy cracks and fills with tears before ending the call.

Chloe replays the last words over and over as the late afternoon slips into evening.

"I am sorry! I am sorry! I am sorry!" she texts repeatedly.

Her text goes unanswered. The chill overtakes her empty feeling and she drives away.

With her tired body sliding into her white pajamas, Chloe pours herself a glass of merlot. Taking a seat on the sofa, her thoughts gather about the previous two days. The evening flows into the ten o'clock hour. As her thoughts deepen, a hard pounding meets her door. Thinking it is Andrea, she hurries to answer it.

"Page, what? Why are you here?" Chloe asks confused.

"Shut up! Unlike others, I am done with this game!" Page says grabbing Chloe's arm, pulling her down the hall and into the apartment. "God damn it, you self-centered brat! Just look at what you have done! You have managed to give hope and take it away in less than twenty-four hours. Do realize what you have done? Congrats. You told someone who has always been in love with you that you love them, and yet you are marrying someone else. You gave Andrea, my best friend, the hope and light she has longed for. Look at her! The one you claim to love!" Page screams.

(Andrea is sitting on the floor at the end of the bed with her knees tucked against her chest. With the short-haired blonde Ridley sitting at her side, Andrea is motionless with a throw covering her shoulders. Andrea stares at the floor as her thin frame shakes.)

"She has been like this since you chose a gown and cake! Yes, the strong and mighty Andrea Parker does feel pain, hurt, and rejection. I guess she is just human! Let me know what it is like not to care! Damn it, none of us know that feeling. Congratulations you broke her! Now get the fuck out!" Page yells taking Chloe by the arm and throws her out.

Chapter Twenty-one

A week has passed, and Chloe, Craig, and her gang are in a sports bar watching a ball game. Craig and Chloe are standing next to one another. Andrea with her date, along with Ridley and Page, enter taking a table across the room. They laugh along with the couple sitting at the table behind them. Chloe glances at the laughter only to find Andrea brushing her date's long dark brown hair that had fallen. Andrea fails to notice Chloe's blue eyes on fire. Craig notices instead.

"Oh, it's just lesbians. I do not know why they must touch or hold hands in public! I do not care that they are gay. I just cannot understand why a woman would want another woman's arms around her."

Because you were never in her amazing arms! Chloe thinks to herself.

Heather is too busy flirting with different guys to pay attention to Andrea's presence.

Trying to refocus, Chloe watches the game. She slightly peeks at Andrea and becomes more jealous with every touch Andrea is giving the brunette.

"Can you order me a whiskey please? I need to use the restroom," Andrea says smiling at her attractive date.

From behind, Andrea passes. Chloe's flaming blues eye brighten at the sight of Andrea passing. Andrea continues toward the restroom.

She is wearing a long sleeve white t-shirt with light gray Atlanta Braves t-shirt over it. She has on faded denims and black leather boots. Chloe is wearing a short skirt with a white silk blouse and heels. The ladylike image Craig insists on. Watching her, Chloe excuses herself and quickly follows Andrea. Chloe forces Andrea into the restroom from behind.

"Jesus Chloe! What the fuck?" Andrea states startled.

Driving Andrea against the wall with a hard kiss, Chloe begins to unfasten Andrea's jeans.

"Stop it, Chloe!" Andrea says pushing her away.

"Andrea, please just talk to me? I am sorry I hurt you. But you do not understand!" Chloe says begging for empathy.

"What do you want me to say?" Andrea raises her voice as she fastens her jeans.

"Just say hello or hi! I miss you and need you!" Chloe says reaching for her.

"Hi? Hello? What does that change? You say you miss me and need me, but if you really want me you would walk out of here arm in arm with me. You would end the engagement and stop living a lie. But you won't! You like the freedom you feel with me, but you are a coward and will not follow your heart. Chloe Conners, I am in love with you. When I held you in the apartment, I was convinced you loved me and wanted to be with me. As usual, I was wrong, thinking I could fit into your world!" Andrea says with tears streaming.

"Andrea, I do love you!" Chloe says holding her arm.

"Perhaps, but not enough to care about my feelings!" Andrea says as her brown eyes shatter with tears.

As their words cease, Heather walks in.

"What the hell is going on in here? Oh, it's the lesbian again. I thought I told you to stay away from her. You Dyke!" Heather says followed by a slap to Andrea's wet cheek.

Andrea is shocked at her aggression. Looking at Chloe, Andrea comments at her lack of reaction while holding her cheek.

"That's what I thought!" Andrea hurries out with tears falling. Ridley runs after her friend. Meanwhile Chloe pushes Heather away and runs out after Andrea.

The cold air chaps Andrea's red cheek as she reaches her Jaguar. Ridley, Page and Andrea's date arrive.

"Dre, what the hell just happened?" Ridley says taking her arm.

"Fucking Heather and Chloe! I did not know she would be here!" Andrea states with anger and tears welling.

Her date touches Andrea's lower back.

"Stop touching her!" Chloe shouts stepping between the brunette and Andrea.

"Go away!" she says removing Chloe's fist balling her leather jacket.

"No! Are you okay? I did not know she was going to do that!" Chloe says showing her resistance.

Catching the five of them off guard, Heather steps through the crowd and punches Andrea in the right kidney knocking her into the Jaguar.

"I fucking told you to stay away from her, nasty dyke! Chloe is straight!" Heather shouts.

The pain splintering through her back and right side, Andrea falls to the wet pavement screaming in pain.

Heather lunges once more.

"Damn it, Heather, have some compassion!" Chloe says kneeling.

Andrea's date kneels touching Andrea's shoulder.

"Stop touching her!" Chloe yells pulling Andrea to her chest.

Heather kicks at Andrea.

"Oh, hell no! I have had enough of you!" Page states wrapping her thick hand around her throat and dragging Heather by her dark hair. She slams Heather against the mural and stands over her. Heather is stunned at the way Page has just handled her.

Chloe tries to lift Andrea from the saturated pavement.

"Stop Clo! I can't feel my legs!" Andrea says reeling in pain.

Ridley kneels and places Andrea's arm around her shoulder.

"Dre, come on find your footing and stand!" Ridley says forcing Andrea to rise.

Chloe and Ridley help lift the embarrassed brunette.

"Okay everyone. It is all over. Come on, Chloe. Playing a good Samaritan time is over," Craig says reaching for her.

"Stop! I'll be right there!" Chloe says swatting his hand away.

The crowd dissipates returning to the bar. Page allows Heather to stand and retreat inside.

Watching Chloe making sure her friends are out of ear shot, Andrea chuckles with disgust.

"Chloe, do you truly love me?" Andrea asks resting against the car.

"With all my heart!" she says caressing Andrea's cheek.

"Then just walk away with me. It is that simple. Leave with me," Andrea begs trying to catch her breath.

"You do not understand," Chloe says staring into her favorite eyes.

"More than you realize. I am in love with you. All I have ever wanted is to be in a relationship, be married, and have a family. I want that with you! All you want is to keep shredding my dignity and heart. I will always only be in love with you, but you do not love

me enough to be happy. So, kiss me one last time. This is goodbye!"
Andrea states.

Andrea places her lips on Chloe's and removes them quickly. The
Jaguar pulls away shortly after.

With her black leather seat reclined, the cold settles in to her shat-
tered heart as she pounds the steering wheel. Andrea's eyes leak and
her thoughts twist and turn like a roller coaster in a dark cavern. She is
heartbroken and enraged at only one person. That person will feel her
revenge in Chloe's March Part Two: The Rise of Andrea